ETHERIC RESEARCHER

ETHERIC RESEARCHER

ETHERIC ADVENTURES: ANNE AND JINX BOOK TWO

SR RUSSELL

MICHAEL ANDERLE

DISRUPTIVE IMAGINATION

LMBPN Publishing
PMB 196, 2540 South Maryland Pkwy
Las Vegas, NV 89109

First US Edition, November 2017
Version 1.01, December 2017

CHAPTER ONE

Jinx twisted as far as she could, but she wasn't able to evade the kick. Her armor protected her from serious damage, but when a Yollin mercenary kicked a hundred-and-twenty-five-pound dog with three hundred pounds of force, the dog went tail over nose.

You all right? Anne asked her friend and partner.

Seeing Jinx flying across the room ignited a part of her she didn't like to acknowledge—the part that didn't mind hurting people. She pushed her speed even higher, faked a punch at the head of the man in front of her, and drove her left foot through his knee joint. She ignored the satisfying scream he gave as he collapsed, and moved to intercept the Yollin focused on Jinx.

Yes, Jinx assured Anne. *My armor is working fine. It's just that guy who got hit in the head with the apple that bit me that time.*

What? Anne sent back, not a hundred-percent focused on their conversation once she was assured Jinx was all right.

1

She dodged the kick the Yollin sent in her direction and grabbed the leg that was still in the air, then flung him ten feet into the three humans who accompanied him.

Jinx had recovered and was circling their opponents looking for an opening. *Some human from years ago. Matrix was telling me about him. He was sitting under a tree, and an apple fell and hit him on the head. Supposedly caused him to write some laws or something. What it comes down to is, if a raging bull hits a china shop, shit's gonna get broken.*

Oh my God, you're hilarious! Anne couldn't stop the smile that resulted from Jinx' banter.

She was reasonably certain that if Jinx had been talking with Matrix about Newtonian physics, there hadn't been any conversation concerning bulls in china shops. There had been a time when Jinx had difficulty understanding nicknames and other odd human phrasings like "hot dogs," but nowadays she seemed to collect metaphors.

"Bull in a china shop" indeed.

Anne ignored the Yollin, who was still tangled with two of the humans, to duck and spin, hands spewing fireballs in an arc toward a new threat she sensed.

"Shit!" Gabrielle hit the floor. "Enough! Stand down, everyone!" She waited for the blast of heated air to subside before she got to her feet. She looked at Anne, who was hiding her hands behind her back. "Was that an invitation to spar?"

Anne shook her head vehemently. "No. Sorry! I sensed someone approaching. Peter surprise-attacks sometimes, so I didn't realize it was you."

"Good reflexes," Gabrielle declared, then surveyed the

carnage in the training room. She knelt beside a Were with his leg bent the wrong way. "This is going to hurt."

He nodded, used his hands to brace against the pull Gabrielle was going to exert, and gritted his teeth. It was a testament to how tough Weres were that he only grunted when Gabrielle yanked on his ankle to straighten his leg so it would heal faster.

"I'm going to have to learn to cover more area with my fireballs …" Gabrielle heard Anne mutter. "I totally missed her when she hit the floor."

Gabrielle straightened from attending to the wounded Were. "Anyone else need treatment?"

A chorus of "No" and "I'm fine" came back to her from the group who had made up the aggressor force attacking Anne and Jinx.

"What happened to the young lady who didn't like to hurt people?" Gabrielle couldn't help but ask as she walked over to Anne.

"Bethany Anne and Jinx," Anne replied cryptically.

"You want to expand on that?" Gabrielle arched an eyebrow.

"Bethany Anne declared that we had to train as strenuously as everyone else. Jinx and I decided that if we had to work out, we were going to go all in and hand out more bruises than we took." Anne stood from checking Jinx. "Jinx took a hard kick that sent her flying across the room, and I always get more aggressive when I feel them getting hurt. Well, Jinx especially, but any of the dogs, really." Anne looked down at her feet for a moment, then back at Gabrielle. "If the dogs get hurt… Well, all bets are off," she finished ferociously.

"Excuse me, Lady Gabrielle?"

While Anne had been talking, Gabrielle had been peripherally aware of the Yollin approaching and Jinx positioning herself between Anne and the alien.

Gabrielle turned to Gre 'Zon. "Yes?"

Bethany Anne had given her the task of recruiting Gre 'Zon. The Yollin was rumored to have contact with ex-military personnel on Yoll, and Bethany Anne hoped Gabrielle could persuade Gre 'Zon to convince those people to join the Etheric Empire's military. Gabrielle had been giving the Yollin a look at some of the training facilities when they had come upon Anne and Jinx's session.

"The animal… It's related to the Empress' companion?" Gre 'Zon asked.

"No way! I have human parents!" Anne exclaimed.

Gre 'Zon looked confused when the human girl answered, and he pointed to Jinx. "I meant—"

Anne cut him off. "You have four legs. Does that make you a lesser being?"

Gre 'Zon clenched his mandibles and bit back the instinctive response that four legs made him *higher* on the social scale. The Empress had decreed that all Yollins were equal, regardless of the number of their legs. "I apologize. I might have been guilty of *grekchlopz*."

"Of *grekta*-what?" Anne was completely confused, and she looked at Gabrielle for clarification.

Gabrielle quickly put the clues together. "He's using a word our implants don't understand, so we're hearing it in his native language."

4

Gre 'Zon's translator allowed him to comprehend the conversation between the humans. He tried again using different words, hoping the human devices could translate these. "Guilty of making assumptions?"

Anne sighed. "Sorry, it just really cranks me up when people define Jinx as an animal as if she's not a person."

"I think it's the lack of hands that does it," Jinx chuffed.

"Wait!" Gre 'Zon held up his hands in supplication. "What did you say?"

Anne took a deep breath, releasing some of her anger as she exhaled. "What part?"

"After 'sorry.'"

"Oh, just something random," Anne replied. "Probably why your implant didn't translate it."

Gre 'Zon reached to his left ear and removed a small device. "Normal Yollins don't have implants. We use a translation device," he explained, then replaced it. He looked carefully at Anne. "Why does your ani...companion make those noises?"

"Noises?" Anne asked. "Oh... She said she thought that not having hands is why others consider her less than a person."

Gre 'Zon clashed his mandibles in agitation. "She said all that?" he asked, looking at Gabrielle as if the older human would give her a different answer.

Gabrielle smiled at Anne's disgusted look. "The Empire's latest implants translate the canines' sounds into that person's default language."

Gre 'Zon looked at Jinx. "And you can understand me?"

Jinx chuffed again, and Anne translated. "Yes. I have an implant that translates every language in the Empire's database. I still have issues with some English words, so I don't always understand what people are saying."

They watched as Gabrielle led the Yollin VIP away. Jinx asked Anne, "How would I talk with people who don't have Empire implants?"

Anne knelt and put an arm over her friend's shoulders as she tried to come up with an option. "If I remember correctly, Bethany Anne captured the Yollins back in Earth's space. To communicate, Yollins wore a harness with a speaker that translated and broadcast to the humans. Why don't we see if we can get something like that made for you?"

"That sounds like a workable option," Jinx agreed, "but the designer had better make it pretty!"

Anne put down some fresh water for Jinx before she headed for her shower. As she let the hot water wash over her and soothe her remaining aches, her mind wandered over the events of the last few months.

She had gone from living at home with her parents to living with her best friend and companion, Jinx. She'd been failing in school, and now she was acing her classes. She'd been suffering from an undiagnosed cancer, and now she was super-healthy and Kurtherian-modified. She'd be called a vampire if she were still on Earth. Anne tilted her face into the spray and used her fingers to comb her dark red hair behind her ears.

Anne almost felt like dancing as the water splashed over her. Bethany Anne had hired her as an Etheric researcher, but to date she had not come up with any ideas that justified Bethany Anne's confidence in her. She wasn't sure how to solve the problem of transferring energy from Jinx' armor, but at least she finally had an idea to explore. With a smile, Anne grabbed her bath sponge, soaped it, and started to scrub the residue of her workout from her body.

Jinx drank the bowl of water almost dry and eyed her dog food, then sighed and laid down while she waited for Anne to get out of the shower. Their sparring match had left her hungry. However, she had learned through uncomfortable experience that eating after drinking a lot while she was hot made her sick. The first time it happened neither she nor Anne had made the connection, but the second time it happened Anne had remembered that this was twice after a workout. As unhappy as she was about it, they tried it once more just to make certain. Sure enough, five minutes after eating Jinx had heaved it all back up.

Yuck!

The next time Anne made Jinx wait until she had stopped panting. Her stomach didn't revolt after eating, so that became their default routine. Jinx could drink as much as she wanted, but she had to wait until she was no longer panting before she ate. Jinx had asked Anne how dogs on Earth would have handled the situation.

"Remember, dogs on Earth are not as smart as you guys, and are owned by humans. I imagine the human would just keep the food away from their dog until they felt it was safe for them to have it."

Jinx ignored the furniture and stretched out on the polished rock floor to leach some of the heat from her body as she waited for Anne. Being kicked across the training room had really pissed her off. She hadn't been hurt, but she had no longer been able to protect Anne's back, and that had left her person fighting everyone by herself. She considered contacting ADAM to ask Matrix to come visit to discuss the issue, but she had a feeling that Anne would want them to try to solve this on their own. This was the sort of thing Bethany Anne had hired her for, after all. Jinx heard the water shut off and figured she'd have about ten more minutes on the rock floor before Anne made her appearance. With a sigh of contentment, Jinx closed her eyes.

Anne dressed in a sleep tee and added a housecoat. Jinx didn't care if she walked around the apartment naked, but there were things Anne just didn't feel right about. Parading around in just her nightclothes was one of them.

She hoped that Jinx would cool down soon. She was hungry, but felt it was inconsiderate to eat when Jinx was overheated. Anne padded into the common area to find Jinx lying on the rock floor. The fact that Jinx' tongue wasn't hanging out was a good sign.

Do you want to eat now or talk first? Anne asked.

Let's start the conversation now. It's not like we'll be talking with our mouths full if we continue during dinner, Jinx teased in reply.

True enough, so where do you want to start?

Well, the armor works fine, but when something big hits me I'm still at the mercy of all that energy. Even if I had crushable impact-activated armor, I'd still have to be able to remain in place for that to work. Jinx practically whined in frustration.

I see only two ways to solve this. One is to put you in some sort of canine power-assisted battle armor, so you have the ...

Jinx did whine this time, cutting off the rest of Anne's comment.

Hey, I didn't say you'd be happy with the solution. I'm trying to go through our options and talk things out with you.

Jinx stood and walked over to lay her head on Anne's leg. *Sorry. Let's get something to eat now, and I'll shut up and listen.*

Anne scratched Jinx behind the ears, smiling at the rumble of pleasure that always brought from her friend. "Grab some of your kibble, but don't overeat. I put two steaks in the fridge this morning to thaw, so you have steak for supper-supper."

Supper-supper?

Ya, as opposed to snack-supper. Your kibble, in this instance, Anne replied as she got to her feet and headed for the kitchen.

I wish I could blow a raspberry like you humans do, Jinx said as she followed Anne, draping her tongue purposely out of the side of her mouth.

Anne smiled when she saw Jinx' funny expression.

Okay, back to the conversation. Armor would be heavy enough to absorb the blows without launching you across a room, or we need to find a solution to bleed off the energy some way.

That's basically what Matrix said when I was talking to him, Jinx admitted as she munched on some kibble.

Did he give you any suggestions? Anne asked. She put on a pan to heat and seasoned her steak. Jinx liked her steak rare with just salt, so the cracked pepper and garlic powder only went on one of the steaks.

None, Jinx grumbled.

"We can't make the energy just disappear," Anne commented aloud as she placed her steak carefully in the hot pan. She liked her meat medium rare, so she put hers in several seconds before she added Jinx' and took Jinx' piece out several seconds before her own. "I imagine your conversation with your brother told you the same thing?"

We didn't go into specifics. I don't have his appreciation or understanding of mathematics, Jinx confessed.

"Well, if I remember my physics, you can change energy's form, but you can't just get rid of it." Anne shook her head slowly as she pondered the problem.

Could we send it to the Etheric place? Jinx gave up on her kibble and laid by the kitchen doorway. Anne would make her wait a few moments for her steak so it would be cool enough to eat without burning her mouth, so she relaxed.

Let me think. Anne was quiet as she flipped the steaks. After ninety seconds she took Jinx' out of the pan, followed by her own thirty seconds later. She added a potato-like vegetable, and her dinner was complete. Jinx' meat got cut into four pieces to make it less messy to eat, and both girls settled in for their suppers.

Even though Jinx had learned to eat slowly, her teeth were much better designed to chew meat than a human's were. Jinx finished her steak in half the time it took Anne to eat her meal. Once they were both done and the dishes had been cleaned up, they moved into the public area and flopped down on the couch.

"Your idea is good. I'm just not quite sure how to accomplish it," Anne said. She spoke aloud for the noise, as opposed to any need.

"I remember people on Earth claiming that certain gems or crystals, and even precious metals, could channel energy. I guess the best place to start would be to get a bunch of samples and see if they react to Etheric energy. If any respond, we'll know they have some sort of connection. Then we'll see if we can get them to transfer energy from this side into the Etheric. To someone who doesn't know what's happening it might look impossible, but we'd just be moving the energy to a different realm."

You could try using that energy to power your Etheric-based combat abilities, Jinx suggested.

"It would be a good idea, but only if we could somehow store it. That way I could tap into it when I need it. I don't need to have fireballs appear, just because someone kicked you, especially if I'm already using some sort of weapon."

Oh, good point. Jinx' ears drooped a little.

"No, it's a clever idea," Anne reassured her friend. "Step one, see if we can channel energy to the Etheric. Step two, find a way to convert kinetic energy into a form that will transfer. Step three would be to see if we can find a way to store that energy so I can tap into it for combat." She smiled at Jinx. "See, we have a plan. Now we just need to see if we can make it work."

Jinx let out a long sigh. *I bet this is going to be boring.*

"It might be," Anne admitted, "but the good thing about it is that we have something to work on. That's what the Empress hired me to do. Even if it is long and boring, at least I'll be able to report on what we are attempting. I've hated it, being hired as a researcher and not being able to think up anything to research. At least now we've got a valid project!" She punched the air with excitement.

Are we starting tonight? After that workout and steak, I'm ready for bed. Jinx yawned, emphasizing her point.

"Yes and no," Anne told her cryptically, then held up a finger to forestall Jinx' response. "Meredith, please contact ADAM for me. I'd like to talk to him for a few moments at most."

Meredith's voice came from the room's speakers. "Message sent, Anne."

She smiled at Meredith's response. "Thanks, Meredith."

Anne knew some people weren't very polite to Meredith. They were part of a "why waste courtesy on a computer?" crowd. But despite knowing that Meredith was the station's EI, Anne took a slightly different view. Anytime she had talked to Meredith the EI sounded just like a person, so Anne thought of her as an EP—Electronic Person—and treated Meredith the same way she'd treat any other adult.

"You're welcome, Anne. Have a good evening."

Before Anne could say, "Thanks, you too," ADAM contacted her.

>> Meredith said you wanted to speak with me?<<

Yes, ADAM, thanks, Anne answered. Knowing the room

had a microphone, along with its speakers, Anne asked, "Can we do this over the speakers so Jinx can hear too?"

"Certainly. I apologize for not thinking of that myself." ADAM's voice now came from the room's speakers.

Jinx looked at the ceiling and barked her agreement.

"You spent several years on Earth, didn't you?" Anne asked.

"Affirmative. I spent several years with Bethany Anne on Earth. Why do you ask?"

"I was hoping that among all the information you acquired from Earth, you might have certain references. I'm wondering about materials that are supposed to be able to channel energy. Even unsubstantiated reports might help us. I'd like a list of articles on materials or compounds that I can test. I need to find something that actually works." Anne tried to be as specific as possible so that she would get the broadest return from ADAM.

"What are you attempting?"

"Jinx can't stand up against more foot-pounds of energy than she weighs. She's tired of getting thrown out of a fight temporarily because of it. We want to see if there is some way to convert that force into energy. I want to discover if we can channel that force into the Etheric as energy, which hopefully would reduce the physical impact on her. I just don't have a clue where to begin. Testing any materials either proven or rumored to channel energy is the best place I could think of to start, and I expect you have a much more comprehensive database than I do."

"You are probably correct. A complete search of everything I have will take seventy-three minutes, eleven seconds," Adam informed her.

"Wow, cool! You must have all kinds of information to go through if it's going to take that long. Thank you so much!" Anne was practically bouncing with excitement.

Careful, please, Jinx warned. *I enjoyed my steak, but not enough to have it revisit.*

Oops, sorry! Anne settled down and stroked the top of Jinx' head, which was tucked against Anne's leg. "ADAM, would you please send your results to my tablet? I think Jinx and I are heading to bed."

"Certainly, Anne. Have you considered that if you are going to be doing a lot of research you might find having your own EI beneficial?"

Anne's eyes practically bugged out of her head at the thought of having an EI, then she sobered considerably. "I don't know. It wouldn't be like Achronyx, would it?" As an example of the difference between an AI and an EI, Anne could detect a chuckle in ADAM's reply.

"No, I doubt very much if your EI would be like Tabitha's. You need to remember that Tabitha was a top-notch hacker before she joined Bethany Anne's group. In *her* reality, computers are things she controls. I don't think that attitude sat well with Achronyx in their early days together, something that undoubtedly helped mold his acerbic personality."

Anne smiled and nodded at ADAM's comment, since she had been the target of Ranger Two's biting wit. Anne giggled to herself, wondering if Tabitha were responsible for her Achronyx' personality quirks. "Who do I ask about the possibility?"

"Consider the request logged. I'll talk with Bethany Anne about your need for your own computer support."

"*Cool!* Thank you so much, ADAM. If the Empress approves, would you share your information files with it?" Anne asked. She wanted the largest possible database, considering all the strange and probably esoteric research she hoped to do.

"There is a slightly weird and somewhat disgusting human saying about teaching your elders to suck eggs. Rest assured that any EI I provide will be equipped with an appropriate database," ADAM assured her.

Anne's eyes went wide once again as the implications of ADAM's statement sank in. "Oh, wow, sorry! I didn't know *you'd* be providing the EI."

"Humans have another saying. 'If you want something done right...'"

Anne completed the saying silently in her head: "do it yourself."

"Do it yourself," ADAM finished.

"Thank you, ADAM, for your help tonight, and for the chance of an EI to work with." Just then the yawn she had been holding back overcame her.

"You're welcome, Anne, and goodnight to you. The results you requested will be on your tablet when you wake." ADAM cut their connection.

"Wow, ADAM giving us our own EI should help a lot," Anne commented to Jinx. "Let's head to bed. We can check ADAM's results in the morning."

Anne stretched as she stood, and with Jinx at her side, she made her way to the bedroom.

CHAPTER TWO

>> Bethany Anne?<<

Bethany Anne, Queen Bitch and Empress of the Etheric Empire, suppressed a sigh at the interruption of her bedtime routine. *Yes, ADAM?*

>> It seems that your Etheric Researcher has her first project. She wants to develop a system that takes energy from our world and transfers it to the Etheric. <<

Is that even possible? And why?

>> She's trying to take kinetic impact energy and transfer it to the Etheric to reduce the energy transfer to a lighter person's armor. <<

Bethany Anne had been braiding her hair for sleep, but ADAM's information caused her to freeze as she considered the implications. *Fuck, could she apply the same technology to our ships?*

>> Unknown. However, if she gets something to work on a small scale it might be possible to get it to work as part of a larger application.<<

Keep me up to date. Bethany Anne resumed braiding her

hair, then stopped again when another thought came to mind. *Why are you bringing this to my attention now?*

>> Anne has asked me to research some information for her, and I can only provide that sort of assistance when we are in the same space as the *Meredith Reynolds*. << ADAM went quiet. He had a bet with TOM on how long it would take Bethany Anne to connect the dots. One point seven-four seconds later...

She needs her own EI.

>> That is consistent with my analysis of the situation. And thank you.<<

For what?

>>I bet TOM that it would take you less than two seconds to come to that conclusion.<<

What were the stakes?

>>TOM will be funding Anne's new EI.<<

You make it sound like she needs something special.

>>Considering her first project, my heuristic analysis indicates a seventy-eight-point-three-nine-percent chance that she will eventually need an AI as an assistant. I want to give her something that can either grow that much or be upgraded as needed to continue to meet her demands.<<

Wow. Bethany Anne took a moment to finish her braid and tied it off with a strand of leather that used to be Michael's. She had to bite her lip to keep the tears at bay. Whenever she used or saw something that reminded her of her missing friend and lover, she wanted to cry. *All right, I will trust you to take care of the situation. Is there anything else going on that I need to know about?*

>>**Nothing that requires your attention before morning.**<<

Right, Bethany Anne sent as she climbed under her covers. *Goodnight. I'll talk to you both in the morning.*

Anne and Jinx rose early, since it was a school day, and after a quick breakfast they headed to class. Anne let Jinx' pressure against her leg guide her while she looked over the list that ADAM had sent her.

Holy crap, she said to Jinx. *I hope Bethany Anne doesn't freak at the cost of this.*

Why, is it a lot of expensive stuff? Jinx asked her.

Almost every precious or semi-precious gemstone known to mankind is on the list, along with most precious metals. I'm going to have to look up some compounds to even know what they are, and those're just the Earth-based elements! In addition, ADAM has a list of compounds and gems he's become aware of since we've been in Yollin space. We're going to need a vault to store everything.

Jinx' ears flattened reflexively at the whine in Anne's mental voice. *How are you going to test them?* Jinx asked her person, then had to react quickly when Anne responded to the question by stopping suddenly.

Anne had noticed the backward flex of Jinx' ears and realized she was complaining more than explaining. She took several seconds to compose herself and give Jinx' question the respect it deserved.

I'm guessing that if we want to route the energy to the Etheric, whatever we end up using has to respond in some way to

Etheric energy. Anne's answer was slower than her normal conversational speed as she thought through the possibilities. *I think I'll have to channel Etheric energy through whatever we test and see what happens. We might find out that the substance we need has no reaction at all.*

How do you figure? Jinx was getting confused now.

If we're looking for something that can move energy into the Etheric, having something that shows little or no reaction might be an indicator that it's moving the energy somewhere. Anne hoped her explanation made sense. She was thinking of the problem in terms of electricity. If you had highly conductive wire that was the right size for the current being sent through it, you didn't notice any change to the wire.

I guess that makes sense. Do you expect the process to be destructive? Jinx asked.

A "Huh" came through their link, then there was a second of quiet before Anne answered, *No, I wouldn't expect so. What are you thinking?*

Jinx couldn't help but wag her tail. She knew she didn't think like a human, but it still gave her a thrill of satisfaction when Anne treated her as an equal. *If you are not destroying things, you can ask to* borrow *the items for testing. Give the Empress' people a list of things you want to test, and ask for so many a week. If you get an EI like ADAM hinted, have it record your tests. Then you just return anything that doesn't work.*

Anne stopped again, purposely this time, and bent to kiss Jinx on the head.

Brilliant! she told her friend, and then they had to concentrate on the crowd of teens heading into the school.

Anne was glad her time in the Pod-doc had tuned up her brain as well as fixing her body, because she was only half-listening to her lessons. The rest of her concentration was devoted to figuring out a way to test samples. It became apparent that she wasn't even *half*-listening when Jinx interrupted her thoughts.

The answer is "perceive."

What?

Mr. Fredericks asked you a question, and the answer is "perceive."

"Perceive, sir," Anne parroted what Jinx had told her.

Anne had an extremely difficult time keeping a straight face when her teacher nodded and said, "I'm glad to see you are paying attention, Miss Jayden."

"Yes, sir. Thank you, sir," Anne said as Mr. Fredericks turned to question a boy sitting in the back. He seemed more focused on whispering to the pretty girl in front of him than listening to the teacher.

Thanks! Anne sent the heartfelt message to Jinx.

De nada, came Jinx' mental voice. *Are you trying to figure out how to test the samples?*

Wait, "de nada?" Anne queried.

I think it sounds better than saying "It's nothing" or "No problem," Jinx replied.

We all have idiosyncrasies, so you're certainly entitled to yours. And to answer your question, yes, I've been thinking about how to do testing. Because of that, I wasn't paying attention, so thanks again. Anne told her as she reached a hand down to give Jinx a surreptitious rub behind the ears.

The rest of the school day proceeded without further incident, and Anne and Jinx eagerly joined the multitudes exiting the facility.

"Meredith?" Anne said quietly after she and Jinx had cleared the crush of students heading to their homes.

"Yes, Anne? What can I do for you?" the station's EI answered through Anne's implant.

"ADAM sent a list of items to my tablet. You can read that, right?"

"Citizens of the Etheric Empire have certain rights to privacy," Meredith told her. "I can access those files with your permission, but unless Security had reason to suspect you of unlawful behavior, I would not do that."

"Oh, that makes sense. It's fine, Meredith. You have my permission to read the files ADAM sent me last night," Anne assured the EI.

"That is quite the list, Anne. I assume you need some information, since you have brought it to my attention."

"Yes. I'm going to need to borrow samples of those items for testing. Who is the best person for me to contact to get them?" Anne asked Meredith.

"Is this in conjunction with your work for the Empress?" Meredith replied.

"Yes," Anne responded. "I guess I should have told you that first thing."

"That's all right," Meredith reassured the girl. "It just becomes more official in this instance. I think Cheryl Lynn would be the best person to contact. She has enough authority to authorize the release of those items to you. Additionally, she probably knows who to contact to acquire them."

Anne skipped a few paces down the corridor in excitement. "That's great, Meredith! Could you message Cheryl Lynn for me, please, and ask her to contact me at her convenience?"

"Certainly. It's done, Anne," Meredith informed the girl. "Is there anything else I can help you with?"

"Thanks, Meredith, but that was all I needed at this moment. Have a great evening," Anne said to the EI.

Meredith had spoken with Anne enough over the past few months to know that Anne didn't differentiate when she talked to people. Four-footed, electronic, or organic, Anne treated them all with the same politeness and respect. So instead of pointing out the ridiculousness of wishing an EI a good evening, Meredith responded with a simple, "You and Jinx also, Anne."

Jinx and Anne had reached their home and Anne had finished her homework before her tablet chimed with an incoming call.

"Hello?" Anne said after touching the screen to accept the call.

"Hi. Anne, right?" a woman's voice said from the tablet.

"Yes, that's me. Is this Cheryl Lynn?" Anne responded.

"Yep. Good guess." Anne could hear the smile in Cheryl Lynn's voice.

"Not terribly difficult," Anne told her. "I was expecting you to call, and I don't get many calls from adult women."

Anne heard a laugh. "Sorry. I'm sitting here with no video nodding my head, and I just realized what I was doing," Cheryl Lynn explained. "Meredith said you needed to talk with me."

"Are you in a secure location?" Anne asked.

"No, and that's the reason for no video. I'm in a restaurant with my two children at the moment. Is that going to be a problem?"

"Not really," Anne replied. "I'll just have to monitor what I say. You know that Bethany Anne hired me to do some work, right?"

"You're talking about your investigative work?" Cheryl Lynn wanted to confirm that the two women were talking about the same subject.

"Yes, and I've got a project," Anne told her. "It looks like I'm going to need some rare and valuable materials for testing. Jinx and I are hoping the testing will be non-destructive, but I'm not prepared to make any guarantees."

"What kind of materials are you talking about?" Cheryl Lynn wanted to know.

With a few swipes of her fingers, Anne forwarded Cheryl Lynn the list that ADAM had provided. "There, you should have the list."

A couple of splutters and a "What the fuck" came from Anne's tablet as Cheryl Lynn read the list.

"Do you need everything on this list?" Cheryl Lynn wanted to know.

"I don't know. It's possible, or I could luck out on the first one. It's why I need to test," Anne said, then continued,

"Jinx suggested we limit things to maybe twenty or twenty-five at a time. I'll return everything that isn't suitable."

"Oh, that would make things much easier." Cheryl Lynn sounded relieved. "Do you have any requirements for what you get when?"

"None at all," Anne said. "Why don't we arrange the list based on what is easiest to get ahold of? That way I can run tests while you're finding the more difficult items."

"That sounds great, and makes a lot of sense," Cheryl Lynn admitted. "Do you have a timeframe for the first group?"

"ADAM commented that I should have my own dedicated computer support, and Jinx suggested we have that computer video-capture all the tests so there will be a record. I'd guess it will be a couple of days before I get a computer, so you'd have that long at least," Anne offered.

"Sounds like a plan." Cheryl Lynn seemed much happier. "I'll start gathering the easiest items. Let me know when you have your computer, and I'll give you what I have at that time."

Anne reached over to give Jinx a one-armed hug, a smile coming to her face when it appeared her project would move forward with minimal difficulty. "Thank you so much, Cheryl Lynn! That would be super. I'll let you know when I'm ready for the first samples. Have a great evening with your children."

"Thanks, you have a good one too. Talk to you later." Cheryl Lynn terminated the call.

CHAPTER THREE

It was two more days before Anne heard anything from ADAM. She had used her spare time to practice channeling Etheric energy into a small cube of stainless steel. Too much energy and it started to glow red in just a few seconds. Not enough energy and she couldn't feel any warmth at all. Anne had spent several hours finding a rate of energy that would warm the steel without making it too hot to handle. She was currently sitting cross-legged on the floor with Jinx' head on her right leg, working on developing her endurance by channeling the energy.

This is boring, Jinx said to Anne. *If you didn't have a free hand to pet me with, it would really suck.*

You chew on your toys to strengthen your teeth and jaws, right? Anne asked.

Yes, do you... Oh! Not fun for you to watch me chew? Jinx hadn't ever thought about how some of her habits might affect her friend.

It's amazing to watch how quickly you can demolish a chew

toy, but it's not the best entertainment, Anne admitted. *This is how I strengthen my control of the Etheric, something I hadn't previously considered doing.*

"Anne?" a voice said from the apartment's speakers.

"ADAM?" Anne asked, confirming of the identity of the caller.

"Yes, it's me," the AI assured her. "I wanted to know if you had a preference toward a male or female personality for your EI."

"Is it possible to change later if I don't like my first choice?"

There was a brief hesitation before ADAM answered. "It's possible if you don't wait too long to make the change, but it may cause difficulty for the EI. It will develop the more you work with it. The longer you refer to it by one gender, the greater the possibility of it developing a gender identity. Imagine how you would react if everyone suddenly asked you to respond as a male."

"Yuck! That would be disgusting," Anne exclaimed. "I didn't realize our computers were that advanced."

"Certain computers are more advanced than others," ADAM informed her cryptically.

"Well, if I need to stick with my initial choice to avoid possible issues, I think I'd be more comfortable with a female personality. At this point in my life I'm not overly impressed with boys," Anne admitted.

"That's fine. This will take thirty-four seconds. Please wait," ADAM informed her.

I wonder what we're waiting for? Jinx asked.

Don't know. Anne shrugged slightly.

This isn't school. I won't grade you, so what's your best guess? Jinx prodded.

I would guess, Anne emphasized the word *"guess," that the programming is complete except for the personality aspect. I think we're waiting for ADAM to load the feminine keys into the personality matrix and boot up our new companion.*

"Anne, Jinx, meet Seshat. Her name is spelled S-E-S-H-A-T, and pronounced 'Say-shat.' She is named after an ancient Egyptian goddess of wisdom, knowledge, and writing. She will be your personal EI. Seshat, Anne is the human, and Jinx is the canine. Both of them have been modified by Kurtherian nanotech, and therefore are significantly more advanced than the norm for their species."

"Greetings," a quiet female voice said from the speakers. "I can locate the radio communication device for Anne, but I cannot identify one for Jinx. Is my search algorithm faulty?"

"No," ADAM's voice once again came from the speakers. "Jinx currently is without such a device. Ten minutes in the Pod-doc will rectify the situation if you'd like your own communicator, Jinx."

"That sounds like a good idea," Jinx chuffed. "Would it be possible for the three of us to talk to each other at the same time?"

"Yes, it would. Anne would need the same ten minutes in the Pod-doc to add another channel to her device," ADAM explained.

"That's no problem," Anne stated. "It does sound like a good idea. How do we set it up?"

"I will have TOM available to let you know what

commands to enter. The Pod-doc is not scheduled for anything tomorrow, so why don't you head there after school and we will get you taken care of?" ADAM suggested.

"Woohoo, sounds great to me. You okay with that, Jinx?"

"Yes, tomorrow after school would be excellent," Jinx confirmed.

"Very well. Just comm me when you are leaving school. I'll get TOM's attention and we can get the two of you taken care of. Talk with you then." With that final arrangement, ADAM closed his communication circuit with Anne's apartment.

"I am sorry that I am causing difficulties," Seshat's quiet voice said from the speakers.

Jinx jumped to her feet and looked at the ceiling, then she looked at Anne. "Is it possible to mount a screen on the wall so we can see Seshat when we talk with her here?"

"That's a great idea," replied Anne, bouncing in her seat with excitement.

"You are not causing difficulties, Seshat," Jinx chuffed to the EI. "We're a pack, and we will all have to learn to make our pack work. Anne and I are still figuring out how to work best as a team, so adding you is not difficult. I just don't think it's right to be talking to the ceiling rather than talking to you."

Anne gave Jinx a hug for her thoughtfulness. She had an idea of her own. "Seshat, would you please see if ADAM could join us again?"

In less than two seconds, ADAM's voice once again

issued from the speakers. "What can I do for you now, Anne?"

"Since we're going into the Pod-doc anyway, is there some way we could add something to allow Seshat to see through our eyes?" Anne asked breathlessly.

"Please wait."

Several seconds later ADAM spoke again. "Sorry, I needed to confer with TOM. He says that it would be possible to place miniature cameras inside your eyeballs that could transmit to Seshat, giving her access to what you see. He recommends the transmission goes through the Etheric to minimize the chance of its being pirated or jammed. In fact, I think we should probably do the same for your implant transmitters. That way you would have a ninety-nine-point-seven-percent secure connection. However, to accomplish all this will require two hours and thirty-seven minutes in the Pod-doc."

Anne looked at Jinx, who responded with a nod.

"That's fine with us," she told ADAM. "Does after school tomorrow still work?"

"Yes, that will be fine," ADAM confirmed. "The Pod-doc doesn't have any bookings at that time tomorrow."

"Excellent!" Anne enthused. "We'll talk to you tomorrow as planned, then."

"Very good. I will use the time you two are in the Pod-doc to make the necessary adjustments to Seshat to let her communicate through the Etheric and decode your video feeds." Once again, ADAM left their communication loop.

"I can't believe you are willing to do this for me," Seshat said after several seconds of quiet.

"Get over it," Jinx growled. "It's not just for you."

Careful there, champ, Anne silently sent to Jinx. *Remember how it took you awhile to get through your puppy stage?*

I do, but what's that got to do with anything? Jinx didn't understand why Anne seemed upset with her.

Seshat's been alive for less than thirty minutes, Anne explained to Jinx.

Oh! She's a newborn. Sorry, I never thought of her that way.

I understand, but yes—she's like a newborn. How we treat her as she grows will probably affect her development and the working relationship we have with her as time goes by. Anne hoped Jinx understood.

She'll grow up faster than a puppy though, right? Jinx wanted to know.

I expect so, but just remember... These next few days especially, what we say to her might have unintended consequences. Just be careful, Anne admonished.

Understood. No jokes or nicknames for a while.

Probably not, Anne agreed, *but if it comes up, just make sure you explain what it is and how it relates to the whole picture. That way Seshat won't be working with faulty information.*

Like telling her a hot dog isn't made of dog. Got it! Jinx drew back her lips and gave Anne a doggy smile.

Or explaining the difference between your smiley face and your growly face. Anne teased.

They aren't hard to tell apart, Jinx complained.

Would a newborn know the difference? That's the question you will need to keep asking yourself for the next few weeks.

"Are you two still communicating with each other?" Seshat suddenly asked.

"Yes, sorry—" Anne started, but Jinx interrupted.

"When I first started talking with humans, a lot of the things they said did not make sense to me. We were trying to figure out how to talk to you without causing you the same confusion I suffered," Jinx explained, thinking that her explanation was close enough to the truth.

"That is very considerate," Seshat responded, "but is it normal for two beings to be able to communicate non-verbally with each other?"

"I think the closest definition you'll find is telepathy," Anne suggested, "and no, it is not common. I seem to have some minor ability, since I was able to communicate with Jinx' dad that way when I was younger. When Jinx and I were in the Kurtherian Pod-doc together, we came out of it with a much-enhanced ability."

"Is that why Jinx asked about a three-way communication possibility?" Seshat wanted to know.

"Very much so," Jinx confirmed. "We'll be working closely together and having a way to communicate with each other without being overheard will have significant benefits."

"Example, please," Seshat requested.

Jinx looked at Anne, who made a "keep going" motion.

"Ummm…" Jinx took a few seconds to come up with what she hoped would be a good example. "Let's say Anne and I are in school. You've been computing data from our research. Your calculations finally finish, but it's only just past lunch. Instead of interrupting classes or waiting four more hours for us to exit school, you could contact us without anyone else knowing. That way we might be able to ask you to run some more data to cross-check the answers."

Making sure that Jinx wasn't going to say anything else on the matter, Anne added, "Or we might be sitting in a crowded restaurant, a location where a public conversation would be inadvisable. Being able to communicate without being overheard would allow us to talk instead of having to wait."

"There appears to be a common thread which indicates impatience," Seshat observed.

"Guilty as charged." Anne laughed. "Our elders say that it is something we will outgrow."

"You admit to being impatient?" Seshat was incredulous.

"Yep. Impatient, emotional, even lazy sometimes. We organic people are guilty of all kinds of illogical behavior. Sorry, but hopefully you'll get used to it even if it doesn't compute for you. If you are having difficulties, you might want to speak to ADAM. He's had a lot of time to observe the oddities of human behavior," Anne suggested.

"That sounds like a surprisingly good idea," Seshat admitted.

"And, please contact Cheryl Lynn and let her know that we will be ready for our first lot of samples the day after tomorrow?" Anne hoped this would make Seshat feel like part of the team.

"Question, should I use her email or comm her directly with the request?" Seshat asked.

"Since it's not an immediate need, I think an email would be a terrific way to start," Anne explained. "If you haven't gotten a response within twelve hours after sending the email, then you might want to comm her."

―――――

It was almost suppertime the next day before Anne and Jinx climbed out of the Pod-doc.

>>Oh wow, the cameras work!<<

Can you monitor the cameras from both of us at the same time? asked Anne.

>>Yes, that is easily within my processing power.<<

Are both our cameras the same? asked Jinx.

>>Yes. Should they be different?<<

Not necessarily, but I think my eyes see things differently than Anne's.

>>Accessing data. I see what you mean. My files indicate that dogs do not see the color spectrum the same way humans do. According to this, you don't see green and red. You are also missing the violet end of the spectrum compared to humans.<<

Really? Anne asked over their new shared link. *Why has that never come up before?*

Probably because we have never needed to discuss color before, Jinx responded. *If it worries you, we can lay out all the colors one day and determine who sees what.*

That might be interesting to do. Seshat, can Jinx see something red?

>>Yes, but the research suggests that she would see a red object as gray. The same thing with other colors. To Jinx, green things would appear more white and yellow. The violet spectrum should also render in gray tones.<<

That is *something we should probably test,* Anne remarked as she started getting back into her clothes. *Did you hear from Cheryl Lynn today?*

>>If your definition of *hear* means did she contact me directly, the answer is no. However, you did receive a box labeled "Samples."<<

Sweet! We can start testing, and now you'll be able to document the tests from different viewpoints, exclaimed Anne. *Did someone install a monitor on the common area wall?*

>>Yes they did, and the monitor includes a camera. Should I have told you that?<<

"I guess we need to come up with some guidelines," Anne mumbled out loud as she thought over the situation.

Jinx put her front legs out and stretched, then stood and shook. *Any changes to our den or any visitors, since I'd smell them as soon as I entered.* Jinx began the list of things that Seshat should tell them about.

That sounds like a good start, I'm sure we'll find things to add as we encounter more scenarios, Anne added.

Once she had dressed Anne led the way out of the Pod-doc, then she and Jinx headed for their apartment. *Now that you have a screen and camera to use you'll need an avatar, Seshat. Do you have any preference?*

>>No, I hadn't even thought about that. Please tell me you don't expect me to use the Egyptian rendering as my avatar.<<

I'm sorry, I never thought to look that up. Is it bad? Anne was curious now.

>>The images have her wearing some seven-pointed thing on her head, and there is no consensus as to what it

represents. Most of the images have her dressed in some sort of spotted animal print.<<

You're right, that doesn't sound appealing at all. I don't know what-all you are capable of, but it sounds like you are able to decide what you like and don't like. Why don't you look at all the images you have access to and find about five you like? Then Jinx and I can tell you which ones we like and help you decide. Anne crossed her fingers, hoping like crazy that Seshat didn't end up liking something horrible.

>>You are still considered a teenager, correct?<<

Yes, why?

>>I was thinking of finding an age-appropriate image, unless I should choose a canine avatar.<<

No! Jinx entered the conversation. *I know you wouldn't really be a dog, but I have an issue with the idea of sharing my den with another canine.*

>>I don't understand.<<

You know we're both modified by Kurtherian tech, right? Anne was thinking furiously about how best to explain what she thought was going on with her friend.

>>Yes, ADAM informed me of that.<<

Despite making changes at a cellular level, it doesn't necessarily make changes to our instinctive reactions. Even knowing that if a spider bit me my nanocytes wouldn't allow it to damage me in any way, I still shudder and want to run if I see a spider. Dogs have a pack instinct, and I'm guessing that seeing another dog in her den would bring out Jinx' alpha tendencies.

Anne is correct. Even knowing you aren't really a dog, seeing a strange dog in my home space would make me want to fight you. I could tell my talking-mind that you were not real, but my pack-mind wouldn't listen. My hackles want to rise just thinking about it. Jinx felt somewhat stupid admitting the problem, but her reaction was what it was.

>>You biologicals are very complicated.<<

If you remember that biological beings are just as likely to react emotionally as logically, we won't surprise you, Anne said while she thought, *Just wait till you have to deal with me during my period.* If Anne were honest with herself she was a lot easier to deal with at that time of the month than many girls at school, and she had her mother to thank for that. Despite the problems and flaws her mother displayed, she had always been an example and a teacher. "Not feeling well is no excuse for bad behavior," her mother would say if Anne got difficult.

Thinking back on it, she wondered if that was why it had taken Jinx to figure out that Anne had leukemia. Anne had been taught from an early age not to let pain and discomfort show. Anne shook her head, remembering how her mother would not allow them to display anything but the best image in public. She made herself a mental note to message her father to see how her mother's therapy was progressing.

Anne and Jinx spent the rest of the trip home in companionable silence.

Since she wanted to start testing now that she had samples, Anne stopped at one of the Guardian Marines' messes to get takeout meals for her and Jinx.

Anne sat in the chair closest to the door and Jinx laid down at her feet. Ever since the evening they had heard one of the Marines mumble about dog hair in his food, she and Jinx had stopped entering the mess any farther than necessary.

"How are my favorite two ladies this evening?" the shift cook asked when they came in.

Anne snorted. The cook looked to be in his forties, and like all the Marines he was in good physical condition. "You must be hard-up if a girl in high school and German Shepherd are your favorites."

Jinx looked around the empty mess. "We're his two favorites at the moment," she said, "and look at our competition."

The cook staggered a step backward, one hand over his heart and the back of his other hand to his forehead. "Ow, ouch, the wounds!"

Anne used her hands to cover her mouth as she giggled at the cook's theatrics.

The man straightened and asked, "What can I get you two this evening?"

Jinx almost had to lick her lip before answering, "I'll have two double cheeseburgers, please. Mayo, but none of that vegetable stuff!"

The cook laughed. "I've seen you sparring and I prefer to keep my appendages non-perforated, thanks. Your burgers won't even get on the veggie side of the line," he promised Jinx.

"I'll have a BLT with a side of fries," Anne ordered when the cook looked at her, "and this will be to go tonight. Thanks."

"White or wheat?" the cook asked.

"Sourdough, toasted and buttered, no mayo on mine." Anne couldn't refrain from crinkling her nose in distaste at the thought of mayonnaise on her sandwich.

"Got it. No mayo with the veggies, no veggies with the

mayo." The cook smiled as he turned toward the kitchen. "Be about five to ten minutes," he told them as he disappeared through the door.

Eight minutes later, with delicious smells coming from the two bags she was handed, Anne and Jinx thanked the cook for their suppers and headed home.

On opening the door to their place, Anne noticed the newly-installed monitor on the wall. Both she and Jinx watched as the camera on the top of the monitor rotated to aim at the doorway.

The monitor displayed equalizer bars that moved up and down with the cadence of Seshat's voice. "Welcome home, Anne and Jinx. Or should I say Jinx and Anne?"

"Doesn't matter, either is fine," Anne said as she set the bags on the coffee table beside a box with her name on it. She headed to the kitchen to grab herself a Coke to go with her supper.

"There are still enough people on the *MR* who see me as an animal that we'd probably have fewer complications if your name was first," Jinx said to the room, knowing Anne would be able to hear her from the kitchen.

"Why not make it random if it's just the three of us, but use my name first if there are other people with us," Anne suggested as she entered the common room with an open Coke in one hand and a plate for Jinx' burgers in the other.

"That works for me," Jinx agreed as she sat with her rear end quivering, waiting impatiently for Anne to unwrap her dinner.

"Implementing RNG if it is just the three of us, and Anne is primary if there are others within hearing distance." The equalizer bars fluctuated as Seshat acknowledged the new directive.

Anne broke Jinx' burgers into bite-sized pieces and put them on the plate for her friend, then unpacked her own supper and looked at the monitor.

Jinx looked at the monitor after she swallowed her first piece of burger. "RNG? What's that?"

"RNG stands for 'Random Number Generator.' It's a subroutine to provide random numbers. If it generates an even number, I'll use your name first. If the result is an odd number, I'll use Anne's name," Seshat explained.

Jinx almost bit her tongue as she tried not to drop the piece of burger she was chewing,

"What's so funny?" Anne could feel the amusement through her link with Jinx.

"Seshat already knows you're odd," Jinx chuffed in amusement.

"For the equation to work, I needed to assign certain values," Seshat stated, "and I assigned those values randomly as well. There was no evaluation of personality."

"It's all right, Seshat." Anne was concerned the EI would think she'd done something wrong. "This goes back to our conversation on biologicals. Our thinking doesn't follow logical paths. When you assigned me the odd factor in your equation, Jinx chose to put a different interpretation on the word 'odd.'"

Jinx had finished her burgers while Anne talked to Seshat. She was heading to her water dish, but she paused. "I was trying to make what is called a 'joke.' I just found it amusing that you assigned Anne as the odd designation."

"Was that incorrect?" the EI asked.

"No!" Jinx was emphatic. "I chose to use one word in a different context. You did nothing wrong."

"It was just another example of our non-linear thinking, Seshat. Do you have some avatar choices to show us?" Anne asked, hoping the EI was satisfied with their explanation of Jinx' attempt at humor.

"I found it a difficult exercise since I had no references to use when examining images," Seshat informed them.

"Did you just select images at random, then?"

"I broke them into age groups first, then selected images at random from each," Seshat told Anne. An image appeared on the monitor. "This one is from the twenty-year-old group." The image was a young woman who seemed like a stereotypical librarian. Hair in a bun, eyeglasses, and a rose-colored blouse that might have been silk but looked shiny enough Anne thought it was satin instead. A black knee-length pencil skirt and black flats finished off the look.

The young woman faded from the screen and was replaced by a different one. "This one is from the nineteen-year-old group."

Jinx looked up, then went back to her water dish. Anne nibbled a french fry as she looked at the picture. This young woman had her blond hair in a ponytail and was wearing a plaid shirt and skinny jeans.

Anne was only partly listening while she reached for her Coke. Seshat said, "This one is from the eighteen-year-old group." Condensation ran down the bottle as

Anne paused with the Coke halfway to her mouth. There was something different about the girl on the screen. It wasn't just the brown hair that looked like it would hit her mid-back if she weren't facing the room, or the black bandeau under a heavy-strand black fishnet top, or even...

"This is from—"

"Wait! Go back," Anne shouted as she half-stood from the couch.

"I do not understand the command, since I have not—"

"Return to the previous picture!" Anne snapped. Then she sagged back onto the couch and finished bringing the Coke to her lips. "Sorry, Seshat, I shouldn't have yelled at you. I just wasn't finished looking at that last picture." Anne looked at the gray eyes under the sculptured brows of the girl who was back on the screen. She shook her head, not fully understanding her reaction. "I like this one."

"You haven't seen all the options," Seshat told her.

"Do you remember my comment about biologicals?"

"If I remember that biological beings are just as likely to react emotionally as logically you won't surprise me?" Seshat waited for confirmation that she had recited the correct information.

"That's the one," Anne said, nodding. "There's just something about her," Anne pointed to the image on the monitor, "that I like. No idea why, I just do. There is no sense in looking at the last two. This is my choice."

"Do you wish to see the other images, Jinx?" Seshat asked.

Jinx took a moment to swallow her water before answering. "Nope, I really don't care what human form your avatar is. I'm good with whatever you and Anne decide."

The static image on the monitor suddenly started to move. As she straightened from the pose she'd been frozen in, the girl's hand brushed the long hair from her face and she smiled. "I am the avatar of Seshat," the young woman said. "It is nice to meet you, Jinx and Anne." The girl smiled again, and Anne watched in fascination as the image grew fangs. "Do I get to have a set of teeth like ArchAngel's?"

Anne was momentarily speechless. Seshat had just asked a question that was unrelated to any of the directives given her. *Oh God,* Anne thought, *please let me get this right.* "Do you think the teeth improve your image?" she asked, trying to understand what motivated the question.

"I have reviewed footage from some of ArchAngel's communications. The appearance of teeth seems to produce a more positive outcome," Seshat replied.

"Are there any common factors involved in those situations?" Anne was pretty certain she knew the answer, so she tried to get Seshat to make the correlation.

"Yes," Seshat answered after a brief pause. "When Arch-Angel displays her teeth in adversarial situations."

Just as I expected, Anne thought to herself. "Do you think the teeth improve your image?" Anne crossed her fingers—she hoped she wasn't pushing Seshat's capability for independent observation too hard. Anne watched as the avatar morphed from fangs to no fangs several times.

"I like the teeth," Jinx inserted into the conversation, opening her mouth to display her own impressive canines.

"From an aesthetic point of view, I don't think the teeth are an improvement," Seshat finally concluded. "However, as previously noted, the presence of fangs does assist in obtaining a beneficial outcome in certain scenarios, both in terms of ArchAngel's communications and looking at human responses to dogs displaying their canine teeth."

"Why don't you use that as your guideline, then?" Anne suggested. "If you encounter a situation where displaying vampire fangs would be advantageous, then by all means show a set of teeth like ArchAngel's."

CHAPTER FOUR

Jinx felt bad about being bored. Anne was working to solve the energy transfer issue, but it was difficult to stay engaged. They'd spent the last three days doing the same things: school, training, homework, supper, test samples.

Jinx was losing the fight to keep her eyes open.

Anne had developed a system. When new samples arrived from Cheryl Lynn, Anne would move them from the shipping box to a plastic storage container. She would take a sample from the storage container, list what it was for the recording Seshat was making, then trickle Etheric energy into it. Seshat would note the reaction, usually a warming of the material, and Anne would repack the sample in the shipping box. Before they had begun Anne had said, 'I think we're looking for a sample with no reaction, because that would mean the energy is going somewhere'.

Jinx managed to suppress a sigh as she stretched and closed her eyes. Maybe she could get away with a short nap. Her feet were twitching as she dreamt of running the obstacle course. She only had to clear the last barrier, and she'd manage a perfect score. She turned the corner…

"Shit!"

The shout and Anne's subsequent frantic movements penetrated Jinx' dream. She was awake and on her feet, her hackles up, before the sound of Anne's cry had faded.

Jinx bared her teeth as she looked for a threat. Anne scrambled from the floor onto the couch and came to a stop almost sitting on the back. Not seeing an immediate threat to her person, Jinx scanned the room. Her gaze was quickly caught by a red glow emanating from a hole in the floor. Only after noticing the glare did she register the heat, along with a hissing and spitting noise. The glare died suddenly and the hissing with it, and within seconds the heat faded also.

What happened? Jinx demanded.

"We had an unexpected reaction," Anne told her as she climbed off the couch and pushed the coffee table out of the way to reveal the hole in the floor.

As Jinx joined Anne she saw a hole in the table, right about the place Anne had been setting her samples while testing.

It burned through the table?

"You are correct." Seshat's voice came from the speakers. "Watch the monitor."

Jinx looked at the monitor that normally displayed Seshat's avatar while the EI was interacting with them. She saw Anne place a sample back in the shipping box, then take a sample from the plastic storage container. Anne placed a red item on the coffee table and said, "Ruby, synthetic industrial." Anne was still for a couple seconds, then she jumped up as the ruby suddenly flared to bright red and burned through the table. The camera continued to record the ruby as it started burning a hole in the rock floor. Jinx watched Anne climb on the couch in the background, shock clear in her expression.

You all right? Jinx asked her person.

"Ya, just startled. I wasn't expecting anything like that," Anne admitted.

They looked at the small hole in the floor.

Is it still in there? Jinx wondered.

"It should be," was Anne's response, "unless it melted somehow."

"How do we get it back out?" Jinx asked.

Anne looked at the hole, rubbed an eyebrow, and pushed her hair out of her face. "No idea." She shrugged.

"Do you have any dowels?" Seshat asked.

"No idea what that is, so probably not," Anne replied.

"Wire coat hanger?" was Seshat's next suggestion.

"Where are you coming up with this stuff?" Anne was curious how the EI was getting her information.

"I ran a search on retrieving small items in restricted spaces," was Seshat's answer. "It shows numerous videos of people with thin objects placing some sort of adhesive on one end and then sticking that to the object to be retrieved."

"What about those metal sticks that had the cooked meat on them that we got from the mess last week?" Jinx almost licked her lips at the thought of the chunks of meat they'd had for their supper that night.

"Skewers?" Seshat asked, the image of metal kabob skewers appearing on her monitor.

"Them," Jinx agreed.

"That's easy. Let's head down to the mess and see if we can get one," Anne offered. She stood from where she'd been kneeling next to the hole in the floor.

"You're here late tonight," Sergeant Thomas Wendville remarked as he saw Anne enter the mess.

"Here to ask a favor." Anne nodded to the man. "Something fell in a crack that I'm trying to get back out." Anne didn't like lying to him, but she knew that telling him the truth in this situation wouldn't be a good idea. "I was wondering if I could get one of the longest, skinniest skewers you have."

The sergeant wiped his hands on his apron. "I don't see why not. Hang tight and I'll see what I've got that will work."

Since they weren't at the mess for food Jinx decided not to enter, so Anne dragged a chair over to the doorway and sat with her friend while they waited for the cook.

"I dug through the pile and found one that's not in the best condition." The cook held up a long skewer that was discolored in places. "You don't need to bring it back."

"Thanks!" Anne felt even guiltier about having lied to the man when he was being so helpful. Despite the discoloration, the skewer came to a sharp point. Anne's forehead furrowed as she inspected it.

"Problems?"

"Just trying to figure out how to deal with the point. Should I try to cut it off?" Anne asked the man.

"What are you trying to get?" he asked.

"A small gold stud." Anne pointed to her ear, implying a lost earring.

The sergeant stood quietly for a moment, then held up a finger. "I'll be right back."

He returned from the kitchen area three minutes later with a small condiment container. "There's a little bit of flour in here. Add an equal amount of water and mix it up well. It will make a type of paste. Wrap a little strip of paper around the end and tape it in place so it forms a tube past the point. Stick the paper in the paste, then try to get your earring to stick to it." The cook gave her a big smile and offered a thumbs-up.

Anne stood and gave the sergeant a hug. "You're the best. Thanks!" she told the now-embarrassed man.

"Ahh, it's nothing," he said, stepping back as he pulled his paper hat from his head. "Just had more years to learn to deal with life's little bumps."

"Well, thanks. You've been a great help." She smiled at the man. "Have a great night." Anne exited the mess and Jinx joined her as they headed home.

After a few failed attempts Seshat said, "I've been researching the type of adhesive you are using. It appears to need time to become effective. I recommend leaving it in contact with the ruby overnight. You can check if it has cured in the morning."

Anne sighed as she stood and arched her back to relieve her cramped muscles. "I'm tired enough that calling it quits now sounds really good, regardless of whether the paste sticks or not."

The next morning Anne woke to a strange sensation. Jinx wasn't in her normal spot against her back.

"Jinx?" Anne called.

Common room, came Jinx' reply. *And don't worry, Seshat ran the simulations and convinced me that I have a very small chance of success pulling the gem from the hole.*

>>A ten-point-three-two-percent chance of success, to be exact.<<

"How did you come up with that?" Anne asked her.

>>I have an image of a canine skeleton in my database. I calculated the depth of the hole and then animated the skeleton to calculate the probability of that structure succeeding in pulling the skewer straight up for the required distance.<<

Anne had wandered from the bedroom to the common room while Seshat answered her question. Seeing Jinx lying on the floor with her nose just inches from the skewer sticking out of the hole, Anne jerked to a stop.

"Seshat, please tell me you have video of this," Anne asked, then bit the inside of her cheek to keep from laughing at her friend.

"What?" Jinx chuffed. She jumped to her feet, then shook vigorously.

"You… You looked like a cat guarding a mouse hole." Anne needed two attempts to answer because she wasn't completely able to hide her mirth. She took a deep breath to calm her giggles. "Come on. I'm not going to attempt this until I get a cup of tea."

"You're addicted to that stuff," Jinx exclaimed.

"Two words. 'Chewy Bones,'" Anne responded.

Jinx looked around the room and saw three different toys that she'd chewed on. "Forget I said anything," she grumbled.

>>Are you two always like this?<<

"Like what?" Anne wasn't focused on Seshat's question at first. "Oh, you mean us teasing each other?"

"Is that how you define the behavior?" Seshat replied aloud.

"Pretty much," Anne set her tablet on a stand so she could see the screen while she worked in the kitchen. "You can tap into that tablet, right, Seshat?"

The tablet flickered once, then Seshat's avatar looked into the kitchen. "Easily," the EI confirmed.

"Good." Anne smiled, then turned to finish putting some water on to boil. Remembering how young Seshat was, Anne hoped she could come up with a good answer. "As for your question, when people live together—or maybe I should say when biologicals share living space—they sometimes don't understand certain behaviors. My morning cup of tea, for instance. Jinx doesn't understand my enjoyment of tea, or how the caffeine affects my body. Likewise, I can't relate to her need to chew on something from time to time. I can understand it from an intellectual standpoint, but I can't relate to it. So, on occasion we'll make comments about each other's behavior in a non-offensive way."

"That was not arguing then?"

"No, arguing usually includes a lot more negativity from one or both parties," Anne explained.

"I think I understand," Seshat responded. "I'll research

the differences between teasing and arguing."

"Just make sure you use valid sources," Anne told the EI.

"Explain, please."

"There have been stories, or possibly rumors would be a better word, about TOM's early days with Bethany Anne. Apparently he could hear entertainment vids that Bethany Anne's crew were watching. Entertainment vids are not known for factual accuracy." Anne chuckled at this point. "The story has it that this led to some misunderstandings between TOM and Bethany Anne."

Anne had made her tea while talking with Seshat, so she lifted her cup and followed an impatient Jinx back to the common room.

"Did it work?" Jinx asked.

Anne ended up slurping some of her tea because it was still too hot to drink politely, then knelt at the skewer. "Let's see, shall we? Fast or slow, Seshat?"

"Considering I cannot find any hard statistics on the adhesive you used, my models indicate that a slow pull has a higher probability of success."

Anne took several deep breaths. "Let's do this, then." She carefully put her finger in the loop of the skewer and slowly lifted as straight as she was able. Both she and Jinx gave sighs of relief when the skewer cleared the hole with the ruby stuck to the end.

Jinx yipped her delight, then sat and looked at Anne. "Do we need to see if you can repeat the effect?"

"Probably not a bad idea," Anne acknowledged. "But

just now we need to get ready for school, so it's going to have to wait until we get home this afternoon."

———

Anne and Jinx didn't get home until suppertime. Mid-morning Anne's tablet had received a message reminding her that she and Jinx were expected for training after school. Anne wasn't happy about it, but since her work for Bethany Anne was supposed to be secret she couldn't beg off by saying she had an experiment to conduct.

A limping Anne followed a limping Jinx into their apartment. They had become such a good combat team that they had held off two Guardian Marine teams. When Peter sent a third team at them, Anne had put together a plan that allowed her and Jinx to break through the perimeter the Guardians had established. Getting out so they weren't surrounded hadn't come without hits. It had been worth it, however, when they'd made their way to a corner of the room and proceeded to eliminate all nine of their opponents.

"You want one of these?" Anne asked Jinx after she'd gone to the medicine cabinet to get a bottle of painkillers.

"That would be great," Jinx confirmed.

"Let's see what we have to cover it with," Anne said as she checked the refrigerator. Anne was pleased she didn't have to try and trick Jinx into taking a pill the way people did with Earth dogs, but that didn't change the fact Jinx wasn't well equipped to swallow pills. They had found it easier to wrap pills in something Jinx could swallow whole. Anne cut a piece of what was considered cheese on Yoll and held it to Jinx to smell.

"This work for you?"

Jinx took a quick sniff. It wasn't her favorite thing to eat, but it tasted a lot better than the pill would if it got stuck in her mouth or throat while she tried to swallow it dry. "It's a lot better than nothing," she admitted.

Anne molded the cheese around the pill, making sure it was completely covered, then offered it to Jinx. Jinx accepted the blob, and threw her head back and swallowed.

Thanks, it went down, she gratefully informed Anne.

You're welcome, Anne responded as she used some water to swallow two of the analgesics herself.

"Can we see if you can get the ruby to burn through the table again?" Jinx asked once the two of them were settled in the common room.

Anne stifled a yawn. "Sure, but let's see if I can *stop* it from burning a hole in the floor this time."

Anne set the ruby on the table and confirmed that Seshat was capturing video of the experiment. She started to feed Etheric energy into the ruby, but at a lesser rate than she had used the previous day. It took longer this time, so both Jinx and Anne were somewhat startled when the ruby suddenly flared red and started burning through the table. Anne stopped the energy flow immediately, and she was surprised when the ruby glow died without cutting all the way through the table.

"Can you activate it again without actually looking at it?" Jinx wondered.

"Dunno, let me see," Anne replied, then focused on mentally sending Etheric energy to the gem. Another red flare, followed by a *ping* as the ruby hit the floor. Anne had cut the energy as soon as she saw the ruby flare, so it was inert by the time it fell through the table to the floor.

"Now what do we do with it?" Anne pondered aloud.

"What about the gun and armor lady?" Jinx offered. "Didn't my dad's person say you could go to her for help?"

Anne reached under the table to pick up the now-cold ruby. "Jean Dukes." She identified the person in question and gave Jinx a hug. "You're right, Bethany Anne did tell us to go to Jean for help if we needed it."

Anne and Jinx took their sample to Jean Dukes' workshop.

"If you'll just make yourselves comfortable, I'll inform Jean that you're here," the young man who led them into an office informed them.

They only had to wait five or six minutes before a no-nonsense-looking woman marched into the office. "Jean Dukes," she said, offering Anne her hand.

Anne had gotten to her feet quickly when the door opened, and she took the proffered hand. "Pleased to meet you, ma'am. I'm Anne, and this is my partner Jinx."

Jinx came up beside Anne and wagged her tail in pleasure as Jean went to one knee and held out a hand in greeting. Jinx sniffed Jean's hand briefly, then pushed her head against the hand. "You can scratch behind my ears," Jinx told the woman.

Jean Dukes put one hand over her mouth to stifle her laugh. "You sound like you're part cat." She snorted, failing to fully contain her mirth.

Jinx growled faintly and moved away from Jean's hand. "See if I offer stress relief again," Jinx chuffed indignantly.

"What?" Jean didn't know what Jinx was talking about.

"It's a proven fact that petting a dog reduces stress in a human," Jinx haughtily informed Jean.

After a few seconds Jean got her expression under control. "How does she know stuff like that?" she asked Anne.

"Probably from talking with Matrix," Anne suggested.

Jinx chuffed her agreement.

"All right. All joking aside, what can I do for you ladies?" Jean inquired.

"Do you have a secure location with a hard surface?" Anne asked.

"How hard are we talking about?" Jean's face wore a puzzled expression.

"As hard as you have, but it needs to be something that won't matter if it's damaged," Anne told her.

Jean raised an eyebrow in curiosity. "Follow me," she said, and led her two guests into her facility. On the way to a secure room, she picked up one of the ten-inch by ten-inch by two-inch pieces of titanium her group used for penetration testing.

Jean led them to what looked like a small machine shop. She waved them through the door, then closed and locked it behind them. "This is as secure as it gets around here. Whatcha got?"

Anne looked around and found a clamp, she motioned to Jean to give her the titanium plate. Anne clamped the plate to a bench with half of it hanging over the edge, then brought the ruby shard from her pocket and placed it on the overhanging section. She figured this way she wouldn't have to worry about it burning through Jean's workbench.

Jean hovered close by, watching Anne's preparations.

"You'll want to move farther away," Jinx warned.

Jean looked at the workbench, then down at Jinx and raised an eyebrow in disbelief.

"No fresh whiskers off my muzzle," Jinx chuffed as she and Anne stepped away from the bench.

Jean looked at where the two of them had moved and then back at the bench. With a shrug, she went to stand beside Anne.

Jean watched the girl and the dog, curious about what was going on. Several seconds went by, then a bright red light and a strange sizzling sound drew her attention back to the workbench.

"*Gott Verdammt!*" Jean exclaimed, using the swear phrase that had been adopted by the Etheric Empire. The small red gem she'd seen Anne place on the titanium wasn't in sight, although there was now a nice neat hole in the metal where the gem had rested. She looked at Anne with raised eyebrows.

"It should be cool in a couple seconds," Anne advised her. "It burns so quickly that it really doesn't have time to heat up the surrounding material."

"What the hell is it?" Jean asked, then looked at Jinx. "Oh, and thanks for the warning," she earnestly told the dog.

Jinx nodded in response, and Anne explained what they'd been testing for. "And then we hit on this. It's a manmade industrial ruby. Add enough Etheric energy, and…" Anne nodded to the piece of titanium.

Jean carefully held her hand over the metal, and when she could not detect any heat she moved closer and looked into the hole. "I assume there's a hole in a table back at your place?"

Jinx snorted. "And about ten inches deep into the floor."

"We weren't expecting a reaction like that, and I was so surprised at what was happening that it took me a couple seconds to cut the power flow." Anne looked chagrined as she confessed to the older woman.

"She had to get a skewer from the mess and put some glue on the end of it to get the ruby out of the floor," Jinx happily informed Jean.

Jean undid the clamp and inverted the piece of titanium over the workbench. After a rap with her knuckle, the ruby dropped out. Jean took the clamp, the ruby shard, and the metal slab and imitated Anne's setup.

"Can you repeat that while I'm watching?" Jean looked questioningly at Anne.

"Sure thing. Three, two, one." Anne pointed at the ruby.

Jean watched the ruby closely. About a second after Anne pointed it flared red and started to quickly burn into the titanium. Once the ruby had disappeared into the metal Jean sensed Anne relax, and the glow disappeared. Jean left everything where it was and dragged a couple office chairs over to the bench. Waving Anne to one, she sat on the other.

"What do you want from me?" she asked the young woman.

"Well, it isn't the answer to Jinx' armor I was trying for, but I was wondering if we could build some sort of weapon." Anne looked at Jean. "I'm thinking something like those laser energy swords in the science fiction movies."

"That's an interesting idea," Jean admitted, "but again, what do you want from *me*?"

"Bethany Anne said I could come to you for help." Anne looked confused.

Jean nodded. "She told me the same thing. The problem is, I'm clueless as to how to help. If you'd brought me a system and said, 'Can we build a weapon from this?' I could possibly help you." She held up a hand to stop Anne from speaking.

"The honest truth is, I don't have a clue how this works. The only Etheric energy stuff I work with was provided by TOM. I can't see, manipulate, or even measure Etheric energy." Jean nodded to Anne to let her know she had finished.

"What do I do, then?" Anne was almost in tears with frustration.

Jean reached over and took one of the young woman's hands in her own. "If it was me?" She waited for Anne's nod. "I'd want my own R&D group. A group of nutty people whose job was to come up with crazy ideas, hoping to find something that works. Remember that what you have here isn't what you were trying to produce."

Jinx stood and placed her head on Anne's leg. "That sounds like a good idea." She tried to project positive feelings at her person.

"How would I do something like that?" Anne wondered.

"I'm guessing your work is going to be top secret, if it isn't already. That means going to Bethany Anne and explaining that I don't know how to help you and you are looking to form your own R&D group. I'll message her and explain why I can't be any help."

Jean took a deep breath, then blew it out and continued, "Then I'd suggest going to William of Team BMW and asking him if he's heard of anyone who'd be a good fit. He's a wizard at what he does. I'd be surprised if he didn't have an ear to the ground, so to speak, about prospective people. Then, once your team is going, my team and I could make time for a brainstorming session or two if you need ideas."

Jean was relieved to see a more positive expression on Anne's face. "No promises on results, however." Jean shrugged. "Might be a case of 'garbage in, garbage out,' but we'll help you if we can."

Seshat, would you please contact ADAM and ask for a meeting with Bethany Anne?

>>Certainly. Standby. ADAM says that Bethany Anne can meet with you tomorrow for fifteen minutes at sixteen thirty, local Meredith Reynolds *time.<<*

That would be great. Thank you, and thank ADAM for me too, please.

>>You are welcome, and done.<<

CHAPTER FIVE

We probably need to get to school early today, Jinx suggested to Anne during breakfast the next morning.

Why's that? Anne smiled at her ability to carry on a conversation with a mouthful of pancakes. She could almost hear a mental snort from her four-footed partner when Jinx deliberately took another mouthful of kibble before answering.

I know there is that saying about asking forgiveness instead of permission, but in this case, since we don't want any issues with leaving school early to make our appointment with Bethany Anne, we should probably talk to the principal this morning.

Anne's hand stopped halfway between her plate and her mouth, syrup dripping off the piece of pancake on her fork. *Crap, thanks! I hadn't thought of that.* She swiped her forkful of food through the syrup on her plate to reload the sweet coating and quickly transferred the dripping yumminess to her mouth.

Well I did, which is why I'm suggesting an early departure.

Anne looked down at Jinx, then at the pancake left on

her plate. She set the plate on the floor and ran her finger-nails down Jinx' back when her friend came over to finish the sticky food. *Thanks! You're the best friend a girl could ask for.*

Jinx settled for a wag of her tail in reply as she concentrated on directing the plate against a solid surface so it would quit moving while she finished licking it clean.

"What can I do for you young ladies today?" the principal asked as his secretary led Jinx and Anne to his office.

Despite his polite greeting Jinx had noticed on past occasions that the principal seemed uncomfortable talking to her, so she left it to Anne to answer the man.

"We have an appointment with the Empress at sixteen thirty today. We'd like permission to skip our last class to ensure we arrive on time," Anne informed him.

The principal looked at Anne and Jinx and asked, "Do you have any proof of this?"

As if Bethany Anne wrote us a note. Anne's mental tone was biting. *Seshat?*

>>Working on it, Anne.<<

Wait, you can hear the conversation?

>>Yes. Along with the cameras you each have, I'm also tied into your implants so I can receive audio from your surroundings. I thought you knew that.<<

Anne noted the concern in her EI's voice. *I might have just forgotten. You're dealing with an organic here! It's not important, it just surprised me for some reason.*

>>You are certain you don't mind? ADAM will be joining the conversation.<<

I don't mind. I didn't remember it being an option, but it will make things much easier now that we don't have to remember conversations to update you later.

"Anne and Jinx have a sixteen thirty appointment with Bethany Anne today," a male voice said from the office speakers.

"Wait, who is this? How are you doing this?" The principal was on his feet, looking around the room.

"My name is ADAM. Besides Meredith, who else do you think could hack into your system to access the internal communications? Also, how many people do you think would be stupid enough to try and fake an appointment with Bethany Anne? I can assure you that once she found out about it, that sort of behavior would not go without repercussions. Sort of the same way she doesn't like jerkwads who waste her time," ADAM finished ominously.

"Er...umm... Right." The principal hooked a finger in the neck of his shirt as if something were choking him.

Anne could feel Jinx' amusement. *I can't imagine his reaction if he knew you could go all Darth Vader on his ass.* Anne looked down to see Jinx' sides quivering with suppressed laughter.

Where did you see that movie?

Matrix and Dio were watching it at Yelena's one day. That's what you want to do with the ruby, right? Make one of those light sword thingies?

Yes, now hush so I can pay attention to the principal.

She focused again on the principal, who was speaking

as he looked at his computer screen. "I'll inform the teacher of your last class that you will be absent with permission."

"Thank you, sir," Anne said as she rose from her seat. "We'd better get going or we'll be late for homeroom."

"Quite. You girls have a good day," said the principal as they exited his office.

With the important appointment looming at the end of the day, time dragged by at glacial speed. When her penultimate class finally finished, Anne had to restrain herself from heading out of school at vampire speed.

Jinx was just as anxious, and quivered with suppressed energy as they left the school.

After a thirteen-minute ride Anne and Jinx exited the tram, and four minutes later they entered the offices where their meeting with Bethany Anne was to take place. Cheryl Lynn looked up from her desk when the two of them came in.

"Anne, sweetie, how are things going with your mother?" Cheryl Lynn asked as she rose from her chair and walked around her desk to offer Anne a hug.

Anne accepted the hug, then took a step back. "She's doing a lot better. The last few times I've visited, Mom reminded me of how she used to be when we lived on Earth. There only seem to be two problems still."

Cheryl Lynn looked into her face. The young woman had always been so polite any time she had dealt with her. "What problems?"

"Mom really doesn't like dogs, and Jinx and I are

together. F'ing-dot-period!" Anne had been looking down at her feet, but when she looked up she noticed the universal expression on Cheryl Lynn's face. *Disapproving mother.* "Sorry, that was crude and maybe a little harsh, but Mom still doesn't seem to understand or accept what Jinx and I mean to each other. And she still won't get an implant." Anne chuckled. "I'm sure it's so she doesn't have to acknowledge that Jinx can talk. The other thing that's an issue is that I've been away from my parents long enough that I have no interest at all in moving back in with them."

Any further comment from Cheryl Lynn was curtailed by the voice of Bethany Anne. "Everything okay?"

Cheryl Lynn saw the leader of the Etheric Empire standing in the doorway of her office. "Sure thing," she answered. "Why?"

Bethany Anne shrugged. "ADAM told me that Anne has been here for several minutes already, and you usually shove people at me trying to keep me on schedule."

"Annnnd just how often do you stay on time once your day starts?" Cheryl Lynn turned the disapproving mother-face on Bethany Anne.

"Don't give me that look or that line of bullshit!" Bethany Anne waved her finger at Cheryl Lynn. "If you'd let me shove those idiots who won't shut up and stick to their allotted time into the Etheric, I'd have no trouble staying on schedule."

Cheryl Lynn sighed. "Heads of government can't just make annoying people disappear."

"Wanna put money on that?" Bethany Anne raised one eyebrow and let a hint of fang show in her smile.

"No!" Cheryl Lynn crossed her arms. "Someone has to

keep you from going overboard, and accepting a wager like that would just give you an incentive."

Bethany Anne stuck out her tongue at Cheryl Lynn. "Too right!"

Cheryl Lynn just shook her head, then looked at Anne and Jinx. They had been turning their heads back and forth like spectators at a tennis match as they watched the two women tease each other. "Why don't you two head into the office and I'll try to get the Empress to join you before her next appointment shows up."

"Ha!" Bethany Anne barked. "When was the last time you checked my calendar?"

Cheryl Lynn looked shocked, then suspicious. She hurried around her desk, dropped into her chair, and activated her display. "*Gott Verdammt*! I assume ADAM is responsible for this," Cheryl Lynn shouted at Bethany Anne's back.

"He only did what I asked him to do." Bethany Anne stopped at the door to her office and turned back to Cheryl Lynn. "The briefing I received about this meeting suggested this was going to require a lot more time than was originally scheduled. Lock up and head home, CL. I'll get us out of here when we're finished." With a wave at the front office, Bethany Anne closed the door behind her and looked at her two visitors.

"Jean Dukes tells me you have something interesting to show me." Bethany Anne remained standing near the door, not certain what form this demonstration would take.

Almost as if she had read Bethany Anne's mind, Anne pulled her tablet and the piece of ruby out of her backpack.

"Do you want a live demo, or the recorded ones?" she asked the Empress.

"The live demo will leave a hole in something," Jinx added with a snort of amusement.

"In that case, let's start with the recorded ones," Bethany Anne suggested as she walked around her desk to take her seat.

>>I can't get a signal to your tablet in the Empress' office,<< Seshat informed Anne over their Etheric link.

"Is it okay if Seshat sends ADAM the files so he can show them for you?" Anne nervously asked Bethany Anne.

"Oh, the office's security measures... Sure, that would be fine," Bethany Anne agreed as she spun her chair a few degrees to allow her to reach a mini fridge. "Coke?" she offered as she reached in to grab one of the bottles for herself.

"That would be great, thanks!" Anne enthusiastically accepted the ice-cold bottle from Bethany Anne. She opened it carefully, took a swallow, and sighed in enjoyment.

I take it Seshat is the name of her EI? Bethany Anne quizzed ADAM as she took a swallow of her own Coke.

>>Correct. Here are the videos of Anne's research.<<

Not only was she happy about this being her last meeting of the day, but Bethany Anne was very pleased that her impulsive act of giving Anne a position as a researcher might be paying off.

Jean had been tight-lipped about Anne's discovery. She had looked out from the screen and held up a finger.

"She's got something scary."

A second finger had joined the first.

"She's going to need help moving forward."

With a third finger now in the air, Jean shook her head.

"I don't have a clue how she's making it work, and even fewer ideas how to help her move forward."

Bethany Anne looked at the woman who had been one of her first recruits. She had never imagined that hiring Jean would have paid off so well. Some of Jean's inventions in her service were legendary.

"What are you telling me?" Bethany Anne was reasonably sure she knew what Jean was going to say, but she needed to hear her say the words.

"She's going to need her own R&D team. I'd imagine they are going to need to be a younger group—people who have mental flexibility."

"Is that a nice way of saying they aren't stuck in a rut?" Bethany Anne chuckled.

"Why did you recruit Anne?" Jean had asked.

"Even though her idea wasn't feasible, at the time she came up with an out-of-the-box solution for a situation," Bethany Anne confessed.

Jean nodded. "She's going to need people who can do that. People who don't have that little voice in the back of their head telling them all the reasons why something won't work. People who are willing to say, 'Fuck it, it doesn't make sense but let's try this.'"

Bethany Anne waited briefly when she saw Ashur come in.

He trotted over, lifted his front paws onto her thigh, and chuffed a greeting at Jean.

"Same to you," Jean said, holding her hand to the camera and flexing her fingers like she was scratching the dog's back.

Bethany Anne waited for Jean and Ashur to finish their greeting, then asked, "You've always been a 'Fuck it' sort of person, so how come you don't want to do this?"

"I could," Jean had agreed, "but it could take months to get results. Do you want me off my other projects for months?"

Bethany Anne shook her head sharply twice. "I'm already worried we'll come across an enemy whose tech is far enough ahead of ours that we'll get our asses handed to us." Bethany Anne had just voiced one of her constant concerns.

Bethany Anne gave her head a figurative shake and returned her attention to Anne's video. Despite thinking she was ready for anything, she felt her eyes widen in surprise when the gem flared red and ate through the table and into the floor.

The video paused and ADAM asked, "There are several hours of video showing the recovery of the gem from the floor. Do you wish to view them?"

"Do they show anything relevant?" Bethany Anne wanted to know.

Anne shook her head, quite happy to avoid having Bethany Anne watch her recover the ruby.

"Okay, let's skip that then, ADAM, and move to the next demonstration," Bethany Anne said, after taking a long swallow of her Coke.

"Stop," Bethany Anne commanded after the new video had been running for about thirty seconds. "Where's the video originating?"

Anne froze in surprise, then turned her head to glance at Bethany Anne. Looking back at the monitor, she realized that Seshat had used the camera in her eye to record the experiment. "Jinx and I needed a little time in the Pod-doc for a communication upgrade to link us to Seshat, so we each had a camera implanted in an eye while we were in there."

I take it you two were behind her getting in the Pod-doc? Bethany Anne asked her companions.

It was such a minor procedure it didn't seem worth bothering you with, Tom responded.

You're more than likely right. It was just unexpected, Bethany Anne confessed. "Please resume the video, ADAM."

Having watched the video from Jean's workshop, Bethany Anne was impressed. "What are you thinking?" She wanted to know what Anne's plans were.

"Well, I was trying to find an energy shunt to reduce the force Jinx has to contend with when her armor gets hit. Obviously…" Anne waved at the screen that had been displaying her experiment, "that isn't what I have. It's powered by Etheric energy, so—for now, anyway—it needs someone who can channel Etheric to make it work. I'll need to experiment to see how long a person can power it, but to do that I have to find some way to contain it so I can conduct tests. That was why I went to Ms. Dukes for help, but Jean says she isn't the person I need for the job. I'm guessing you want to keep this secret, so she said I'd need your permission to find my own, umm…staff, maybe?"

"Staff, team, flunkies—it doesn't matter what you call them. And you're right, you need the Anne version of Team BMW." Bethany Anne held up a finger, a slight smile showing on her lips. "Team BMW would be a good place to start. Not that they have time to help you, but Marcus and William might know or have heard of people you could interview and recruit. If they don't have any recommendations, talk to Frank Kurns. He's almost magical when it comes to ferreting out that sort of information."

Anne had been expecting something like this after visiting Jean, but the scope of what she needed to do suddenly hit her like a physical blow.

Jinx noticed the change in her person and leaned against Anne's leg to offer silent support. "If… No, I guess it's *when* we find someone, what do we do? Bring them to you?" Jinx asked her dad's person, taking over from Anne momentarily to give Anne a chance to recover from whatever was bothering her.

Bethany Anne drained the last of her Coke, giving herself a couple seconds to consider Jinx' question. She shook her head, disgust on her face. Noticing Jinx' reaction to her expression, she held up a hand. "That wasn't directed at your question. It just brought to mind how extremely limited my time is nowadays. I think your best option would be to have Barnabas be part of your final interview process." Bethany Anne stopped as she noticed a strange expression on Anne's face.

"That's Ranger One, Tabitha's boss?" Anne asked into the sudden quiet.

Bethany Anne nodded. "Yup, that's the one."

"Umm, wouldn't it be easier to ask Tabitha instead?"

"Easier, possibly, but as you said, your work is going to be classified. You don't need a Ranger-Ranger, you need someone who can read minds. Tabitha doesn't have that particular skill but Barnabas does, so he can ensure you recruit people with the appropriate ethics."

"Oh my God!" Anne jumped from her chair, both hands going to the top of her head. "I'll be hiring people!" She looked at Bethany Anne with an expression of near-panic. "How do I pay them? How *much* do I pay them?" She shook her head. "I don't think I'm ready to be someone's boss."

Bethany Anne reached down and pulled two more Cokes from her refrigerator. Offering one to Anne, she said, "Calm down! Here, take a sip and sit back down. The man I mentioned, Frank Kurns? Well, he's amazing with stuff like that. I'll get ADAM to ask him to contact you."

"Message sent." ADAM's voice came from the room's speakers.

"Great." Bethany Anne smiled. "Glad I could solve that so easily."

The sound of a person blowing a raspberry came from the speakers.

"No fair," Jinx groused. "I can't do that, but an AI can?"

Bethany Anne spent several more minutes helping Anne develop a plan of action. Once they had everything settled, Bethany Anne rose and motioned for Anne and Jinx to follow her to a spot in the room big enough for all three of them to stand together. "Hold still and concentrate on a big empty spot in your apartment," she said, taking Anne's arm with one hand and laying her other hand on Jinx' head. Seconds later the office of the Etheric Empire's Empress was empty.

"Can you do that?" Jinx asked Anne after Bethany Anne had transported them to Anne's apartment and then transported herself out.

"No idea," Anne answered. "Want to try?"

Jinx' ears standing to full alert and her tail wagging like crazy were all the answer Anne needed. She reached down and carefully grasped the scruff of Jinx' neck. "Seshat, if we're not back or you don't hear from us in thirty minutes, contact ADAM and have him tell Bethany Anne we got lost in the Etheric somewhere."

Before Seshat could respond to the order, Anne focused on the spot in the park where she and Jinx had found Christina banging her head on a tree.

"Well, this is going to make it more difficult to keep track of her," Seshat said to the empty apartment.

Anne and Jinx were both drenched within seconds, and Anne's shoes filled with water. She had managed to port them into the park as planned, but the sprinkler system was on and their arrival area was in a shallow depression, currently filled with standing water.

Jinx shook the water from her coat. Deciding that the

sprinkler was fun in a messy sort of way, she ripped a mouthful of grass from the ground and tossed it into the air. Then dashing to what they now called "Christina's tree," she ran a loop around it and raced back to Anne.

Anne just stood there, clothing soaked and water streaming down her face. She watched Jinx, chuckling at her friend's antics, but then the ramifications of what she had just accomplished sank in. She fist-pumped and, ignoring the soggy ground, knelt to throw her arms around Jinx. *"We did it!"* she shouted.

"I don't think I did anything other than coming along for the ride," Jinx chuffed. "And while I don't mind the water, what if this had been on fire or something else was happening here?"

Anne sank back, her expression morphing from giddiness to shock as the ramifications of Jinx' comments hit home. "Oh my God!" she exclaimed, her hands going to her cheeks. "I never thought of that."

Jinx couldn't refrain from shaking her head as some of the falling water trickled into her ears. "You could ask ADAM, or I could ask my dad to find out if Bethany Anne has a procedure she follows."

"Would your dad keep quiet about it?" Anne voice dropped to a whisper. "I'm not sure I want the Empress to know how stupid I was."

"I see I won't need to contact ADAM," Seshat's avatar was on the monitor when they returned, arms crossed on her chest and a look of disapproval on her face. "What happened to you two?" Seshat had noticed the "drowned rat" look of both Anne and Jinx.

Anne sighed. "Just a second, let me towel Jinx down." She followed her words with action as she took a towel from the linen closet and began to dry Jinx. "The short version is, I can port through the Etheric. We arrived at the park while the watering system was active, which explains why we are wet. Jinx then pointed out that we could have arrived during a catastrophic event, which means we were fortunate this time. I need to figure out a safer way to do this."

Anne gave Jinx a brief hug once she got most of the water out of her coat. She headed to the bathroom to correct her own situation, hearing the voices of Jinx and Seshat in the room behind her.

CHAPTER SIX

The following morning Anne spent several more hours testing samples while she waited for All Guns Blazing to open. From their reputations, she figured that would be the best location to find William and Marcus on a Saturday afternoon. Anne flexed her shoulders, stretching out her tight muscles, and put her two containers of samples away.

Jinx jumped down from where she had been napping on the couch. "Time to go see Team BMW?" She wanted to confirm they were going out for a while.

Anne nodded. "Yes. I can only take doing this testing for so long, then I need a break. If we walk instead of taking the tram, we should get there just about the time they open."

Jinx' tail started to wag as they headed for the door. "Good. Since I was asleep most of the morning, the exercise will be welcome."

Anne reached down to stroke Jinx' ears. "Sorry it's so boring," she told her.

SR RUSSELL & MICHAEL ANDERLE

They exited the apartment and headed for the most famous bar in this sector of space.

Jinx gave Anne's hand an affectionate lick. "No, I'm sorry. I ended up falling asleep while you were doing the testing. You're trying to find something that will benefit me, after all. You'd think I could stay awake for it."

"Don't worry. If I had to watch someone do what I'm doing I'd fall asleep too," Anne confessed.

"How do you keep doing it, then?"

"Every time I get bored or frustrated with the lack of progress I visualize you getting kicked several feet across the room. Then I imagine the possible outcome if that were to happen in a fight for our lives. The thought of you being seriously hurt or possibly killed because I got bored with testing..." Anne's explanation came to a halt as she sniffed and brushed a tear from her eye. "Let's just say I don't ever want to be responsible for you getting hurt."

Jinx leaned into Anne's leg. "Good," she told the girl. "Keep testing then until you find the solution. I don't want to find out what it feels like to see you get hurt because I wasn't there to protect your back."

"Deal!" Anne exclaimed, then smiled down at Jinx. "We're quite the pair, aren't we?"

Jinx was silent for several seconds while she padded along with Anne. "We're soul mates," she said earnestly. "Not in the way humans like to claim their lover is a soul-mate, but in the way we think, the things that are important to us. We just mesh."

Anne stopped, and when Jinx turned back to her she knelt and hugged her tightly. After several seconds, she released Jinx and leaned back to look at her. Seeing the same sort of love and devotion she felt for Jinx reflected, she gave Jinx a quick kiss on the nose.

Anne rose and, content in each other's company, they quietly resumed their trip.

All Guns Blazing was already busy by the time Anne and Jinx arrived. They were standing inside the door, not quite sure how to proceed, when a waitress hurried over to them.

"What do you want, sweetie? You know I can't serve you alcohol," the waitress remarked.

"Why's that?"

"You're with Jinx. That means you must be Anne, and I know you're not old enough to drink."

Anne wasn't here to drink, but she pouted playfully anyway.

"Oh, don't give me that look," the waitress said. "It is not my fault there are only seven dogs on this rock."

"Hey, does that mean I'm famous?" Jinx wondered.

"I don't know about famous. 'Rare' might be a better word." The waitress smiled down at the sable German Shepherd dog.

Jinx's ears drooped a bit. She'd hoped to be famous, like her parents.

Anne reached down to scratch Jinx' neck in reassurance. "You can be rare, like a precious gem. I'm sure famous will come in time."

"I guess it's a good thing I wasn't planning to order a drink." Anne looked at the waitress. "I need to get in touch with Marcus and William. I was hoping to find them here."

"That was a good guess," the waitress agreed, and smiled. "Let me go check and see if they're here yet." She pointed to a bench inside the door. "If you will just wait here?"

Jinx waited until Anne had settled on the bench and then planted her butt on Anne's feet. The waitress was gone for several minutes, but the two of them didn't really notice the passage of time. Watching the constant stream of different beings entering and exiting the bar kept them entertained.

They stood as the waitress emerged from the stream of traffic. "They are all in the office arguing over who brews the best beer," the waitress informed them.

"Oh, I wouldn't want to interrupt them if they are busy," Anne confessed.

"Busy!" The waitress put a hand to her face and turned away briefly when she couldn't contain a snort. "They are not busy, this is just their pastime. The three of them have turned betting and arguing into a hobby and an art form."

"I thought brewing beer was their hobby?"

"No, brewing is something they all take very seriously. Betting and telling bullshit stories are their hobbies," the waitress informed her with a smile. "You two just follow me."

The waitress led them to a door in the back area of All Guns Blazing, where she knocked and announced, "Anne and Jinx here to see you."

"Well, let them in," a male voice called. "They can't see us through the door!"

Anne and Jinx looked at each other as they heard laughter from the men in the room. *Did they think that was funny?* Jinx wondered.

Don't know, but we need their help so let's be polite, Anne suggested.

Polite! Laugh at lame ass jokes, got it, Jinx commented as the waitress opened the door and waved them in.

A distinguished-looking man stood as Anne and Jinx entered the room. "Greetings! I'm Marcus. Please forgive these two reprobates their lack of manners. They don't know any better."

"Hey, I resemble that remark." One of the men chortled.

"Word!" said the other, holding his hand up for a fist-bump.

"'Resemble Man' is William, and 'Word Man' is Bobcat." Marcus pointed at each as he made the introductions.

"Jinx," Anne said, indicating her friend. "And I'm Anne," she continued. "We appreciate your help."

Marcus waved her to a chair, and sat back in his own seat. "Oh, I'm going to like you."

"Why?" the man introduced as Bobcat asked.

William cleared his throat and looked sheepishly at his friend. "She said she appreciated our help, not that it was nice to meet us."

"Word." Marcus imitated Bobcat before dissolving into laughter.

Bobcat started to give Marcus the middle finger, then quickly pulled his hand into his lap when his brain caught up to the fact they had a strange young woman in their office. "Sorry," he offered. "Working with and for Bethany Anne, you…"

"People don't have to be polite or politically correct around Bethany Anne. Our Empress could and *does* give lessons in the art of swearing," Marcus finished for Bobcat, who couldn't figure out a polite way to complete his sentence.

Anne bit the inside of her cheek to keep herself from giggling at the men, who all looked uncomfortable. "No problem," she assured them. "Both of us have been around the Empress enough to know what she's like. In fact, she was the one who suggested we come to you for help."

Bobcat, William, and Marcus glanced at each other, mild concern in their expressions.

Jinx found it all very amusing, but figured she and Anne might have better success if these men weren't more concerned with protecting their tails than helping with the situation. "It's William and Marcus she suggested we talk to," Jinx informed the men.

"Great!" Bobcat said, jumping up from his chair and heading for the door. "I'll go get us all something to drink."

"I'm a loyal subject of the Empress," Anne commented as Bobcat opened the door.

"What's that supposed to mean?" he asked her, somewhat perturbed that she might imply he wasn't loyal to Bethany Anne.

"Coke, not that other stuff." Anne smiled at him.

"Oh, I try to avoid that conversation altogether. I drink beer!" he exclaimed proudly as he left the room.

"All the time?" Anne asked the two men she had come to talk with.

"Nope, he doesn't drink while he's sleeping," William told her with a huge grin.

"Well, that's good to know." Anne smiled back. "He probably would have needed an intervention otherwise."

Marcus started to laugh and pointed his finger at Anne. "I knew… (chuckle) I was… (chuckle) Going to like you!"

Anne held up her hand for a high-five with the rocket scientist, then turned to William. "Bethany Anne suggested you might know someone I could interview for a research job."

"What kind of research?" William scratched a raised eyebrow.

"I could tell you, but then I'd have to kill you," Anne said to the man.

William's smile slowly faded as it became clear to him that Anne wasn't entirely joking. "Ouch," he remarked, looking at the ceiling briefly. He let his gaze come back to Anne. "What can you tell me without going to extremes?"

Anne pursed her lips as she tried to think of a way to explain what she was doing that wouldn't violate Bethany Anne's edict that her work be secret. "Let's just say that I'm working on stuff that might compare to your ESD project. I need someone really creative to help me develop it."

William's eyebrows rose so far they almost met his hairline. "You're shitting…" William flushed with embarrassment and "me" came out as a whisper.

Jinx chuffed her amusement and put her muzzle on the table. She looked at William. "'We shit you not' is the proper response, I think," she told the shocked man.

William sat back in his chair, looked up, scratched his head, and blew out a long breath. "I've heard rumbles from the school's machine shop courses. A guy named Stevie, and something in Russian that sounds like Kas-eean-ov. Supposed to be graduating in a couple of months and is blowing all his classmates out of the water, so to speak."

"Sounds like a person I want to talk to," Anne enthused, glad that it looked like she was moving in the right direction. "Please let us know if you hear of anyone else who might possibly meet our criteria."

With Jinx by her side, Anne exited All Guns Blazing and headed toward their apartment. After turning into a secondary tunnel that led into the interior sections of the *Meredith Reynolds*, they had travelled about eighty feet when two aliens stepped from an intersection in front of them to block the passageway. A quick glance over her shoulder showed Anne that a third alien now blocked their retreat.

The one Anne assumed was the leader, because he was the one who spoke, growled, "Give us the animal, little girl, and no one gets hurt."

Anne looked at the camera, one of the hundreds Meredith used for monitoring interior spaces, and raised an eyebrow.

"Dat's not gonna do youse any gud!" the second alien told her, holding up a device that Anne guessed must be some sort of jammer.

We're getting held up by the Three Stooges?

Who are they? Jinx wondered

>>The Three Stooges were a slapstick comedy team on Earth, active from 1922 until 1970. And their device isn't

blocking Meredith. I wish there was a display screen at your location so I could show them my fangs.<<

I didn't expect it would be able to block Meredith, Anne commented. *That's part of the reason I called them the Three Stooges. And you're absolutely correct, this would be a great situation to show off your fangs.*

You need to show me these Three Stooges dudes when we get home, Jinx proclaimed.

Only if you promise you won't go around saying "nyuk nyuk nyuk" afterward, Anne told her.

"Quit stalling and give us the animal!" the leader shouted as he pulled a rod of some sort from behind his back. It reminded Anne of the fighting sticks she had seen the Marines use in practice.

Taking a deep breath to center herself, Anne firmed her stance as she had been taught.

"You guys just need to go while you can," Anne said in a quiet voice.

"The animal!" the alien with the jamming device yelled, pointing at Jinx.

"Look," Anne spat, quickly losing patience, "you've got so many things wrong it's not funny."

"One," she said, holding up a finger, "Jinx is a four-legged person like some of the Yollins."

"Two," another finger joined the first, "your jamming device isn't working."

"Three—"

Can I have the boss guy? Jinx' increasing anger created an underlying growl in her communication.

Sure thing. You take the two in front of us, and I'll take care of the guy at our backs.

"You can't possibly think you can kidnap a citizen of the Etheric Empire and get away with it," Anne finished.

"Annnnnd," she stretched out the word as she extended the fourth finger, "someone's definitely going to get hurt!"

Jinx had crouched slightly as Anne ticked off the numbers. She heard Anne's *Go* in her mind at the same time she heard "Get hurt" with her ears, and she shot forward. She laughed to herself as she thought of a sign Anne had shown her. It was a German Shepherd Dog and the words, "My dog can reach the fence in 2.9 seconds. Can you?"

Three quick bounds and a coiled-spring leap later, she had the arm holding the weapon in her jaws. She shook it like a fish on a line as she bit with all the force her nano-enhanced jaws could generate. As she had planned, her attack spun the alien, which carried her away from the second one.

Then she heard Anne shout, and a sickening scream.

She had planned to release her first enemy and come back to engage the second alien. The first alien, however, was whipping his arm back and forth and she saw that if she timed it just right... *Now!* She let go of the first alien and her momentum took her right into the second Stooge. *Chewy bones,* Jinx used her canine version of *OMG,* her person was funny.

Anne spun toward the attacker behind them as she held up a fist glowing a sickening green color. "Five!" she shouted. *"No one* hurts Jinx!"

With that she flung the ball of green flames down the hallway. She had been completely serious when, after missing a ducking Gabrielle, she had remarked that she'd need to practice her attack technique. Instead of separate fireballs, this new type held together until just before it reached its target. That was when it acted like a shaped charge penetrating a barrier. A cone of incredibly hot energy particles burst from the ball, and the alien screamed as the particles hit his center of mass.

Anne had commandeered a test dummy for her attack practice. Remembering the damage she had done to the poor dummy, she knew her target was dead—or as good as. With her target down Anne turned to support Jinx, but she wasn't needed.

The wounded alien leader tried to backtrack around the corner, but came to an abrupt stop with the barrel of a Jean Dukes Special in his face.

"Going somewhere?" John Grimes asked, his nose wrinkling in disgust as the alien voided himself.

Jinx had her second alien on the ground and was standing on his chest, teeth firmly clamped on his throat. She hadn't bitten through his skin yet, but Anne could see indents from the pressure Jinx was applying.

Should I rip his throat out? Jinx asked.

Remember what Bethany Anne said about Barnabas, or herself even? I'm guessing they need live people to read minds, Anne suggested as she walked over to pick up the fighting baton that had been dropped when Jinx had attacked.

What's the human term? Oh, ya. "Party pooper," Jinx groused.

Baton in one hand and another green ball of energy

forming in the other, Anne looked down at the alien. "Jinx is going to release you now. Do anything stupid and you'll wish I had let her rip your throat out!"

John Grimes, Queen's Bitch, motioned with his weapon back down the hall to where Anne and Jinx were with another alien.

"I'm injured. I demand medical assistance," the alien whined, cradling the arm Jinx had shredded against his body.

"Really?" John asked, then before the alien could register the movement John advanced and kicked him in what would be the knee joint on a human.

The alien screamed and dropped to the ground, writhing in pain and trying to grab his joint with one hand while still protecting his already injured arm.

"Did you want to demand anything else?" John asked as he stood over him.

The alien moved his head back and forth in the gesture he had been told indicated a negative response to humans.

John sighed, wishing he'd been able to hurt the alien a little more before he cried "Uncle." He wasn't normally a vindictive person, but for anyone who came into Bethany Anne's empire, especially her backyard, and tried to jack one of Ashur's puppies?

He'd make an exception!

He grabbed a harness across the being's chest and dragged the whimpering male back to where Anne and Jinx stood.

Bethany Anne was trying very hard to be a good Empress. When Meredith had informed her that there appeared to be an issue of some sort between Anne, Jinx, and three aliens, she had sent John to investigate.

When Meredith had updated her that Anne and Jinx were fighting the aliens, Bethany Anne had smiled and continued reading the report in front of her.

When Meredith reported that Anne had disappeared and Jinx was extremely upset, she closed the document, asked for a visual of the location, and stepped into the hallway near All Guns Blazing. Enough was enough.

Jinx was frantic. She and Anne had taken out the aliens with ease, but then someone had said, 'This one's dead' and Anne had clutched her stomach and disappeared. Jinx cast about desperately for some scent of Anne, some hint of where she had gone. Someone stepped close to her, and she spun to bite the interloper. Her top jaw was caught in an unbreakable hold, and it sank through her panic that she had attacked Bethany Anne.

"I'm willing to forgive you *once* for that attack. Try to bite me again and I'll throw you tail over nose across the room. We clear?"

Jinx was now under enough control that she noticed the red in Bethany Anne's eyes.

"Clear," Jinx acknowledged.

"What happened?" Bethany Anne looked around at everyone for answers.

>>Anne is at home. She appeared in the common room and ran to the bathroom. While I don't have a camera of my own in the bathroom, the view from her camera is a closeup of the toilet, and she seems to be depositing partially digested food into it.<<

Jinx barked sharply to get Bethany Anne's attention. "Seshat says Anne is at home, throwing up in the bathroom."

"We'll be back," Bethany Anne told John and the others who had congregated at the scene, then grabbed Jinx' fur and stepped into the Etheric. Having previously traveled to Anne's apartment, she knew where she was going. She just stopped to look out and confirm the area was clear before she brought them out of the Etheric.

Seshat had been monitoring Jinx' camera, and when it showed the outside of their apartment she activated the front door. Not even a second later Bethany Anne and Jinx rushed into the apartment and headed for the bathroom.

Anne didn't know how long she'd been heaving the contents of everything she'd eaten all week into the toilet. Well, not all week, she admitted to herself, but it sure felt that way. Lunch and breakfast had come back up, then an eternity of dry heaves and tears had joined that mess in the toilet.

"You finished yet?" A quiet voice finally penetrated at a level she could understand. She felt a hand rubbing her back, and Jinx pressed so tightly against her side it was like they were glued together.

"Bethany Anne?" Anne asked, turning her head slightly to see the Empress... No, this wasn't the Empress, this was her friend Bethany Anne. Anne took a hand from the rim of the toilet and hugged Jinx tightly.

"I killed him," she whispered through a new bout of misery and tears.

"And hopefully you'll feel this bad the next time you have to kill someone," Bethany Anne told the girl.

"What?" Anne took her face from Jinx' fur and turned shocked eyes to Bethany Anne.

"Killing is necessary sometimes, but if it no longer bothers you, you're not human anymore." Bethany Anne reached for a towel on the rack next to the sink and handed it to Anne.

Anne took the towel with a weak smile, and used it to wipe the sweat and tears from her face. "Does it still bother *you*?" she asked Bethany Anne.

"Yes and no." Bethany Anne turned and sat on the floor, her back against the tub, and gazed at the young woman in front of her. "I had to reconcile a long time ago that some people are so warped or evil that they have to be permanently removed from society. It doesn't bother me to do that, because I know that I'm protecting a lot of innocent people in the process. What *does* bother me is that those people have let themselves get so sick or twisted that they force me to act to protect my people."

She watched Anne for an indication her message was understood. "Those aliens tonight...why did you fight?"

SR RUSSELL & MICHAEL ANDERLE

"They were after Jinx!" Anne answered through her clenched teeth.

Bethany Anne nodded. "You see? You didn't attack them for shits and giggles. They made a decision that forced you to act. Now, you could have given Jinx to them —" Bethany Anne held up a hand to cut off what she was sure would be an angry retort from Anne. "Or you could have run away," she continued, still holding her hand in the air, "but you decided long ago that you would do everything in your power to protect your friend, right?"

Anne had calmed while Bethany Anne was talking. She looked at the older woman and carefully nodded her agreement.

"Sometimes 'everything in your power' means someone's going to die. You *will* learn to cope with it, but I pray you never get to a point where you enjoy killing someone."

"Do the Weres?" Anne wondered.

Bethany Anne was quiet for several seconds while she pondered the question. "I really don't know. You'd have to ask Peter or Jennifer. I think they take pride in the strength and skill that lets them triumph." She shook her head slowly. "I don't know if they *enjoy* killing someone."

"It's a strange situation, isn't it?" Anne commented.

"What is?" Bethany Anne encouraged her young friend to talk.

"Being happy that you protected a friend. Being glad that your training and skills allowed you to triumph, yet feeling upset that it resulted in killing someone."

Bethany Anne nodded, then stood and extended a hand to Anne. "You're right, it *is* strange. However, you have every right to feel satisfaction in your skills and accomplishments. You two have been extremely dedicated, and have worked hard to acquire the skills you displayed tonight. That's not going to stop me from assigning you a security team, however."

"*What?*" Anne froze, staring at Bethany Anne.

Bethany Anne had shrugged off stares from Michael, so this one was easy to ignore. "We've just found out that Jinx, and I imagine any of the dogs, are targets. Sooner or later rumors of your project are going to surface, which will make you a target in your own right. I'm not going to find myself banging my head against the wall one day, trying to figure out why I wasn't smart enough to assign you a security detail. That's an oversight I'm fixing now. I'll talk to Peter and find out who he'd recommend for a Guardian Marine detail for you." She pointed a threatening finger at Anne. "No arguments."

Anne grabbed her toothbrush and loaded it with toothpaste, wanting to get the nasty taste out of her mouth. Before she turned on the water she asked, "Do I at least get a say in who the team is?"

"Do you have someone in mind?" Bethany Anne was curious now.

Anne spat the toothpaste from her mouth. "No, I just want to know what happens if there's someone we don't get along with."

"Oh," Bethany Anne said, and nodded. "If you find someone who rubs you the wrong way, just let us know and we'll assign someone else. You finished?"

Anne rinsed her mouth. "Am now."

"Follow me," Bethany Anne told her, and headed for the front door. It opened on Scott and Gabrielle standing outside the apartment. "I don't think any of us are 'happy,'" she made air quotes, "needing security, but at least we can arrange it so you get along with your team." Bethany Anne stepped between Scott and Gabrielle and put an arm around each of their necks, pulling them close.

Gabrielle stuck her tongue out, while on the other side of Bethany Anne Scott displayed one of the goofiest smiles Anne had ever seen.

Anne raised an eyebrow, pointed a thumb in Scott's direction, and told the two women, "Wow, he's got talent."

"Shush," Gabrielle said in a stage whisper. "If his ego gets any bigger, he won't fit through the doors."

Jinx listened as all four humans laughed at Gabrielle's comment and let out a sigh of relief. Her human looked like she was going to be all right.

CHAPTER SEVEN

Monday morning saw Anne and Jinx walking to school in silence. Anne was tired, and Jinx was worried. Anne hadn't slept well the last two nights—it was difficult to sleep when nightmares woke you up screaming.

Anne had ended up with three different nightmares. The first one she understood and had almost expected: a replay of her attack on the alien. The other two were worse, and she just wasn't sure which was more disturbing. In one, she didn't kill the alien and the Stooges got away with Jinx. Then they strapped Jinx down and cut pieces from her to try and clone her. That was the first time she woke screaming.

The other dream was disturbing on a completely different level. She was on an alien planet, and every time she looked at an alien it was instantly engulfed in flames and turned into a charred skeleton. Dream-Anne had tried closing and covering her eyes, but it didn't help. Somehow she could still see the aliens. Male, female, child—it didn't matter. She had no control over who got burned. What woke her screaming from that one was that she saw a **Playground Ahead** sign and couldn't stop walking.

Seshat says that almost everyone who deals with this kind of thing needs counseling to get better. After she said it Jinx cringed mentally, afraid of being told to mind her own business but needing to try to help her friend anyway.

Sounds about right. Anne reached down to gently rub one of Jinx' ears, acutely aware of the love that had given Jinx the courage to say those words.

You're not mad?

If you had a badly broken leg and I told you that you needed surgery to have it heal correctly, would you be mad at me? This conversation made Anne realize how little they had talked since the incident. Just the fact that they were communicating again made her feel better.

I don't think so, Jinx answered.

Anne grabbed the tip of her tail and gave it the briefest of tugs. *I try to be at least as smart as you are.*

School was…interesting. That was the only word for it. With her Kurtherian enhancements, Anne could hear most conversations held anywhere near her—all the conversations in the room she was in, actually. She wished she could conduct a poll. It would be interesting to find out if she were more admired or feared. By lunch period Anne had decided "feared" was in the top spot. It wasn't the comments that led to this conclusion, it was that no one had been brave enough to ask about what had happened.

I don't know whether to laugh or cry, she told Jinx when they had found a place to sit and eat lunch.

Well, you also kicked the asses of those Weres earlier this year. I'm guessing it all adds up, Jinx reminded her.

Anne chewed the bite of pizza she had just taken, then nodded her head. *I'm not going to pretend to be happy or proud of beating up or killing people, but I think I prefer being able to defend and protect myself. It beats living with so much fear you can't even talk to someone you've known for months. I don't want to be a bully, but how many undies would need to be changed if I threw one of the harmless fireballs into the middle of this room?*

Jinx almost choked on the piece of bratwurst she was eating.

>>Research indicates there are laws against behavior that can create mass panic.<<

Anne burst out laughing and couldn't help but notice some of the people nearest her flinch at the sudden sound. *Thanks, ladies, I needed that. What do you say we get out of here and see if we can't track down that Stevie dude before class resumes?*

The shop teacher, Mr. Jenkins, was middle-aged and overweight, and caused both Anne and Jinx to wrinkle their noses at the slightly rancid odor he emitted. He showed them to his office and invited them to sit.

"Why don't you come back here as soon as school's out?" he suggested. "That time slot is the graduating class, and I can introduce you to Herman. He's very promising."

SR RUSSELL & MICHAEL ANDERLE

Anne looked at Jinx, then back at the teacher. "Herman? We were told we should talk to a guy named Stevie?" Anne's confusion turned her sentence into a question.

Mr. Jenkins' expression morphed from mild interest to condescending. "People will always try to put one over on you," he informed them.

"I got the name from a very highly recommended source," Anne remarked calmly.

"Look," he sighed like he had to explain something obvious, "*she*," and he emphasized the pronoun, "insists on being called 'Stevie,' but her name is Stephanie Kasyanov." Mr. Jenkins had a sneer on his face and pronounced the name with derision.

Something about this guy is not right. I'm going to let you do all the talking, Jinx told her friend.

"I take it you have a problem with Miss Kasyanov?" Anne acknowledged Jinx' message by asking the question.

Mr. Jenkins snorted. "What *isn't* a problem? Girls are supposed to take Home Ec, not shop. She's one of those shifter types, and if you believe the rumors, she doesn't like boys—if you get my drift. I could ignore all that, but you did catch her name, right? Ca-See-En-Off," The teacher stretched and distorted the girl's name. "She's a Ruskie! Can't trust them Ruskies any further than you can throw 'em."

Anne just sat there silent and stunned. How the *H-E-double-hockey-sticks* did this man ever get a job as a teacher? She finally got her mind into gear. "Is the principal aware of your concerns?" she asked the man.

"Hardly!" the man spat. "He salutes a rainbow flag, not

Old Glory." Mr. Jenkins looked at the American flag prominently displayed on the wall of his office.

"Why work here, then?" Anne was truly curious what his answer would be.

"Someone's gotta keep an eye on 'em," he said, putting a finger to the side of his nose.

Anne wasn't sure what the gesture meant, but she thought she remembered seeing something like it in a movie. She nodded and tapped the side of her own nose, then stood. "I'd better head out before I'm late for my next class. See you right after school."

Mr. Jenkins returned her nod. "You'll be glad you came to me for help."

Leaving Mr. Jenkins' office, Anne ignored her next class and headed straight for the school's office.

What's his problem? Jinx asked as she padded beside Anne.

Just a sec, let me see if I can get them all. Anne was quiet for a few steps. *I think he's a homophobic misogynistic xenophobic redneck. I might be missing one.*

Jinx chuffed her amusement. *Are those all real words?*

Yes, they are. If he's also a racist, which I suspect he is, then he hates everyone except white American men.

How do people live like that? Jinx was incredulous.

Anne shook her head. *Human history is full of people and societies that almost made a religion out of beliefs like that.*

Have I told you lately that humans are confusing?

I don't think I've ever argued the point, have I? Anne turned and stuck her tongue out at Jinx.

Real mature, Jinx teased.

It's been a rough couple of days. I'll take my distractions where I can find them.

Jinx froze, her ears and tail drooping, then started moving again, hurrying to catch up to Anne. *Sorry, I wasn't thinking.*

It was Anne who stopped this time, and she knelt to be at Jinx' eye level. *Don't worry. You tease about humans, but I think dogs truly have a different thought process. It just means it's not your fault.*

That doesn't make me feel better when I say something that is painful for you.

Just ask yourself if you were trying *to make me feel bad. If the answer is no, then I'm not going to hold it against you.*

"Why aren't you in class?" was the greeting they received when Anne and Jinx entered the office.

"We've just come from a...let's call it a discussion, with Mr. Jenkins, the shop teacher. It was disturbing enough that I felt it warranted informing the principal," Anne told the secretary, then sat in one of the chairs lined up against the wall.

"Disturbing in what way?" the secretary asked.

"In a way I don't feel comfortable discussing in a public place," Anne declared as she swept her gaze pointedly around the open and very public area.

The secretary gave Anne a disgusted look, but touched a button on her desk. "Sir? Anne Jayden is here to talk to you. Something about the shop teacher, Mr. Jenkins. Yes, sir. Thank you, sir," the secretary finished, then stood.

"Follow me," she said, leading Anne and Jinx to the familiar office of the principal.

Once Anne was seated with Jinx sitting next to her, the principal steepled his fingers. "What can I do for you ladies?"

Seshat, can you break into the school's system to run video here in this office? Anne sat, slightly embarrassed, as the principal raised an eyebrow at her.

Seshat?

>>What? Oh, sorry, you were serious? I thought you were being facetious! Meredith's *gravcarts* could hack into the school's system. Do you want the footage from your conversation with Mr. Jenkins?<<

Please.

As the video from her meeting with the shop teacher ran, Anne began to get concerned. The principal wasn't reacting to the footage. No, that wasn't quite correct. He was reacting, but he was showing exasperation, not shock, anger, and outrage.

"You knew!" were the two words Anne uttered once the video had reached its end.

"Most of it, despite Mr. Jenkins' beliefs to the contrary," the principal admitted.

"Why is he still employed?" Anne wanted to be furious, but she had a sneaky feeling this was going to be one of those things she couldn't do anything about.

"He is an excellent teacher, for the most part," the principal said quietly but earnestly. He made an expansive gesture with his arm, trying to encompass more than just his office or even the school. "We're in a closed ecosystem. It's not like I can run help wanted ads in London, Madrid,

Barcelona, Paris, and New York to hire a replacement. A lot of parents don't feel comfortable with an alien teaching their children, so I'm stuck. I have to make do with whoever's available—however upsetting or distasteful that may be."

Anne was somewhat shocked by the revelation, and her mouth formed a silent 'O.'

"I'm sorry to have wasted your time," she said, once she got her vocal chords working again.

The principal shook his head. "I truly appreciate that you felt strongly enough to put yourself out there and bring it to my attention. Just... As I said, we're living in a closed system. If it's any consolation, I've heard the same reports of Miss Kasyanov's brilliance. Instead of having to deal with Mr. Jenkins' personality, just come back here when school's out. I'll get a message to Stephanie to report to the office once she's done for the day."

CHAPTER EIGHT

Stephanie "Call me Stevie" No-Middle-Name Kasyanov was having a bad day. She could speak English fluently, but trying to understand it as a subject in school? English made no sense at all! Shop was her last class of the day, and she was normally able to submerge herself in the design, plans, blueprints, and machining the class entailed. Today, however, Mr. Jerk-ins was being more of an idiot than normal, if that were possible. And the sour grape that topped off the whole mess? She'd been handed a note as she left her English class to report to the office before she left school. She had to devote some energy to fighting the urge to throw back her head and howl.

"Psstt! Want to go to the school dance with me on Saturday?" Mark Holmes whispered.

Stevie took a quick look around the classroom. The last thing she wanted was for the Jerk to give her detention. "Not any more than the last three times you asked me," she whispered back.

"Ahhh, man, you're killing me!" Mark added some theatrical embellishment by putting a hand to his chest.

Alerted by Mark's loud response, Mr. Jenkins turned to glower at the young man. "Just who is killing you, Mr. Holmes?"

Mark refrained from looking sideways at Stevie, since he could feel her staring daggers at him. She was gorgeous, which was one of the reasons Mark wanted to date her, but she had a very nasty temper if you upset her.

"No one, sir. I was just trying to get this assembled before the end of class, and it's not fitting together properly." Mark held up several bits and pieces from his current project as proof.

"I suggest you recheck all your measurements, then," Mr. Jenkins advised. "You have probably cut a piece to the wrong size if it does not fit together."

"Yes, sir. I'll get right on that, sir." Mark cursed under his breath. Now Mr. Jenkins would watch him carefully for the rest of the class, and he wouldn't have any more opportunity to try to talk Stevie into going out with him.

Jennifer wiped her face with one of the towels stacked around the workout area and watched as Pete put two different Guardian Marines teams through their paces. Always a curious person, Jennifer made her way to his side. "What're you doing, oh fearless leader?"

Peter had years of practice living with the pranks the Guardians and Marines liked to perpetrate on each other. So, he didn't even twitch when Jennifer spoke, since he'd been aware of her approach. "You've trained with Jinx and Anne, right?"

"Sure. I've been shifting and teaching canine combat techniques to Jinx," Jennifer confirmed.

Peter turned his head enough to look at Jennifer, but kept an eye on the sparring teams. "Did you hear they got attacked walking home from All Guns Blazing?"

Peter waited for Jennifer's gasped, 'No! What happened?'

"Three bistok-shit-stupid aliens tried to dognap Jinx. She and Anne objected strenuously, and they ended up with one dead, one running, and one subdued by the time John arrived."

"Oh, shit!" Jennifer exclaimed. "Who racked up the kill?"

"Anne. She hit one of them with some sort of Etheric energy grenade."

"How's she holding up?" Jennifer asked, concerned about Anne's psychological well-being.

"Don't know for sure," Peter admitted. "I haven't seen her in here since the incident."

"Poor kid. That's going to be difficult for her to cope with. What's that have to do with all this?"

Peter turned back to the sparring match. "Bethany Anne has decided Anne and Jinx need their own security."

"And?" Jennifer asked.

"Winning team gets the assignment," Peter stated, with a sigh that made it sound like it was an obvious conclusion.

Jennifer laughed. "Oh my God! You're an only child, right?"

"Everyone knows that. What's that have to do with anything?" Peter gave Jennifer his complete attention.

"No girlfriend either?" Jennifer persisted.

"My dating options have been somewhat limited," Peter growled. "What's that got to do with picking a security detail?"

"Which of these guys is going to follow her into the ladies' room? Who's going to go with her when she needs to go shopping for underwear? Do any of them know to suggest Midol and a heating pad at that time of the month?" Jennifer ticked off the points on her fingers as she made them. She finished with, "Think! If you had a younger sister, would you be comfortable with an all-male security detail?"

Peter scratched the back of his neck as he pondered Jennifer's words. "We don't have any female Weres available."

"No, but you have several female Marines. What about those cousins? You know, the ones Bethany Anne recruited from the Israeli Defense Force?" Jennifer felt bad that she didn't know the women's names.

Peter clapped his hands to get the attention of the sparring teams. "Take a break, guys. I've just been informed," he pointed his thumb at Jennifer, "that I need a mixed-gender security team." He looked at the Marines. "What are the names of those cousins who are former IDF?"

"You're talking about Abigail and E," one of the Marines offered.

"'E?' What kind of name is that?" Peter couldn't help asking.

"Her real name is Ethel, but she doesn't like it. She

complains it's too old-fashioned, so she asks everyone to call her 'E,'" the Marine explained.

"Does Abigail use her full name, or does she prefer Abby?" Jennifer asked.

"She might *prefer* Abby, but I think she uses both," another Marine told her.

"You're right. It seems to depend on who she's talking with which name she prefers," the first Marine added.

"Thanks for your time. That's it for now, since it looks like I have a couple ladies to talk to," Peter said as he started walking away from the workout area.

Anne and Jinx were heading to the office to meet with Stephanie when Anne caught sight of the familiar profile of Peter Silvers and stuttered to a stop. She heard a whispered "Oh, crap" just before someone bumped into her. "Excuse me," the same girl's voice said, and Anne felt a hand on her back as the girl pushed around her. The girl had only taken two more steps when she stopped dead with a muttered, "What the puck?"

"You weren't expecting to see Peter either, I take it?" Anne asked her compatriot.

"You know him?"

"Yep. Instructor, sparring partner, slave driver... Not sure what he's doing here, though," Anne admitted. She looked carefully at the girl and when she paid attention to her senses she caught the scent of Were. "I'm gonna make a crazy guess that you're Steph—"

"*Stevie!* I go by 'Stevie,'" the girl interrupted her.

"—anie Kasyanov." Anne wasn't going to let the girl upset her.

"How did you know..." Stevie's voice trailed off. She'd been so concerned about the summons to the principal's office that she hadn't been paying attention to her surroundings. When the girl in front of her had come to a quick stop, she had pushed around her without noticing the dog at her side. "You're Anne, right?"

"Yup, and this is Jinx," Anne said. She motioned to her companion, then held out her hand to Stevie. *I'll call her Stevie if it makes her happy, but I'll be thinking Stephanie every time I say it,* she sent to Jinx. "I'm the person you're hurrying to the principal's office to meet."

Stevie held out her hand automatically but said, "Do you mind if I withhold judgment on the 'nice to meet you?' And do you really spar with Peter?" she asked in the same breath.

"I don't mind, and not as much anymore." Anne followed Stevie's lead and answered both questions. "Shall we?" she asked as she nodded toward Peter and the office.

Now that she was paying more attention to her surroundings, Anne noticed three adults standing by the wall on the other side of the office doorway.

One Were, two humans, Jinx advised when she realized her friend had noted the group.

"Hey, Peter! What's up?" Anne asked when they got to him.

Peter smiled at the young woman and her canine companion. Both had improved so much in their training since he'd first met them. "Let's move this out of the hallway, shall we?" he suggested as he held the door open.

Once all seven of them had entered the office, Peter looked at Anne and Stevie. "I take it you have business with the principal?"

"We did, but I'm not sure it's valid anymore," Anne replied. "He was supposed to introduce me to Stevie here, but we bumped into each other in the hallway."

"Well, let's check with him," Peter said while he scanned the office for the man in question. "Then if he needs to do something else, he'll be free to go."

The secretary disconnected from the call that had occupied her when everyone entered. "Ahh, Anne and Stephanie…"

"Stevie!" Stevie ground her teeth in frustration.

"Your official records show your name as Stephanie," the secretary commented in an officious tone.

"Only 'cause my mother filled them out when I entered school," Stevie mumbled.

Just then the door to the principal's private office opened. The man stuck his head out and looked around the room. "Ahh, Miss Kasyanov and Miss Jayden," he called, then paused as he noticed the girls' proximity to each other. "Have you met already?"

"Yes sir. We bumped into each other in the hall, literally," Anne proclaimed.

"Well, good, then. Is there anything else I can do for you?" the principal queried.

"No sir, we're good, I'm going to invite Stevie to my place and we can talk there." Anne smiled at the young woman she hoped was brilliant enough to help her with her research.

The principal looked at Peter and the three adults with

him. "Guardian Silvers, do you need my assistance in some way?"

Peter shook his head. "No, thank you. I was just here to find Anne. As you can see," he waved a hand at the young lady in question, "I have succeeded."

"Very well, very well. If everything is settled here, I have some other business to take care of," the principal said. He re-entered his office to grab a tablet from his desk, and as he exited he nodded to everyone and walked briskly into the school's main hallway.

Anne looked at Stevie. "You okay coming to my place for a few so we can talk?"

Stevie pulled her tablet from her shoulder pack. "Sounds good," she acknowledged as she typed. "Anne Jayden, right?"

"You know how the school won't stop calling you Stephanie? Well, they won't stop calling me 'Miss Jayden.' It's just Anne," she explained.

Stevie froze and took a reflexive sniff of the air.

Anne laughed. "We don't need to drink blood anymore, so we don't stink the way vamps used to. You should know that by now."

"I know." Stevie looked sheepish. "It's a reflex."

"No problem. Let's head out." Anne and Jinx started down the hall toward the school's exit.

When they headed out, the man with Peter started walking a few steps ahead of the group. Peter stayed with the girls, and the women followed two steps behind. Without thinking about it, Anne took the turn she and Jinx normally used for their walk home. She'd only taken one step when she felt a hand on her shoulder.

"You don't dart off without your security," Peter informed her, pointedly looking at the man who had been walking in front of them.

Anne looked at Peter, shock morphing to indignation. She held up a finger. "One, Jinx and I gave up taking the tram, so this is our regular route home. Two, no one has mentioned I *have* security, let alone what to do with them."

Peter looked at the young woman he had helped train and felt proud of what he and his team had shaped. Anne wasn't angry, nor was she afraid to stand up to him. She didn't feel responsible for any breach of behavior, and wasn't going to let him make her feel guilty about it. "Bethany Anne told you she was going to assign you a security team, correct?"

Anne scowled but nodded in agreement.

Peter's hand swept out to include the three people now arrayed around them. "Meet your sec—"

"Ett!"

Peter was shocked when Anne raised a hand and cut him off.

"Yes, Friday Bethany Anne said I needed a security detail. This is Monday, and this is the first I've heard on the topic since then. You can introduce them all you want, but I'm not taking blame or feeling guilty about taking my normal route home. I'm sure if you check with Meredith she can verify this."

>> I can tell them.<<

I know you could, Seshat, but as far as I'm concerned it's up to them to know or find out before they start complaining.

"Well, I was going to wait until we reached your place."

Anne stopped Peter again when he took a breath to continue. "Sounds like a plan."

CHAPTER NINE

With Anne giving the occasional instruction, the group made their way to her and Jinx' apartment.

"I have Cokes, water, and what passes for sweet tea here in Yollin space," Anne announced from the entrance to the kitchen. She almost laughed when she looked back into the common room area. She wasn't set up to entertain five humans at a time. The men were trying to defer to Stevie, who was having none of it.

Anne grabbed two chairs from her dinette set and dropped them at the doorway to the common room. "Here's some more seating. It's normally just Jinx and me, so we've never had a reason to acquire more furniture."

Since no one had voiced a preference for a beverage, Anne hunted around until she found the six-pack carrier the Coke bottles had come in and filled it with six cold bottles from her refrigerator.

Watching this group is more fun than watching the Three Stooges. Jinx laughed in her mind as Anne rejoined the small crowd in her common room, her spare hand dragging one more chair from the dinette. Anne understood what Jinx meant when she saw her five visitors still milling around. Stevie was standing by one of the dinette chairs, but didn't look comfortable enough to claim it. The men were looking like they were afraid Anne's comfy couch would bite them.

"Jeez, guys, it's just furniture. It's not booby-trapped, I promise." Anne set the six-pack of Cokes on the coffee table, extracted two bottles from it, and offered one to Stevie. She pointed at the chair Stevie was hovering by and said, "You take that one." She arranged the chair she had just brought beside it and sat down.

"Peter, you take the other chair. That leaves you three," she motioned at the two women and the gentleman still standing, "to share the couch."

Jinx waited as people got settled in the seats Anne had specified, then walked over and sat by her person. She looked at Peter and chuffed, "I know why Stevie is here. Why don't you tell us why you're here?"

Peter looked at Jinx, and then at Anne. "You are both aware that BA has decided you require a security detail." He waited until he got an affirmative reply from them. "We've decided, at least for now, to start you off with a Guardian Marine team." He pointed to the middle-aged man. "This is your Were, Arthur Connors. Your Marines are cousins, and I'm going to let them introduce themselves," Peter informed her as he pointed to the women. "They were Israeli Defense Force on Earth, so they really know their business."

Anne leaned forward and offered her hand to the Were.

Arthur reached over and shook her hand from where he sat.

"You barbarian," one of the women exclaimed. "Being able to turn furry is no excuse for bad manners."

"What?" The Were, Arthur, looked completely confused.

"You stand when you're introduced to a lady," the other woman chimed in.

Arthur looking at the two women, whose expressions were like disapproving school matrons'. "Oh," he said, and stood. He looked somewhat sheepish as he shook Anne's hand. "My mother taught me better, I promise. I just wasn't thinking," he confessed as he released Anne's hand.

Once Arthur had reclaimed his seat, the woman next to Anne offered her hand. "I'm Abigail Himmel, but you can call me Abby if you'd prefer."

"I'm her older and wiser cousin E Brenner." The second woman stood and offered her hand above Abigail's head.

Anne stood to shake the proffered hand.

Before Anne could ask, Jinx looked at the first woman. "'E?' I have problems with human language sometimes, but I thought I was getting better. I've never heard the name 'E' before."

The second woman sat back down at the end of the couch and sighed. "I'm named after my great-grandmother Ethel." E took a breath and blew it out in disgust. "'Ethel' is just so old-fashioned, and I used to get teased about it in school. Once I finished school and applied to the IDF, I started telling people to call me 'E.'"

"Okay, Arthur, Abby, and E." Anne nodded at each in turn. "For those of you who don't know, this is Stephanie

Kasyanov, though she prefers to be called 'Stevie.'" The young woman blushed. "She's here for a job interview. Time will tell if she becomes part of the team."

Peter cleared his throat to gain everyone's attention. "I'll try to keep this short and make it sweet," he said, looking at Anne. "You will have one of these three," he motioned to the Guardian and the Marines, "on-duty and near or with you at all times when you are in the interior spaces of the *MR*. This includes school, mess, and any other interior areas you are visiting or working in. If or when you go to the outer edges where aliens have access, you will take at least two of your team with you. And before you make a fuss," Peter pointed his finger at Anne, "these are Bethany Anne's rules, not mine."

"Okay, let me see if I've got this straight." Anne held up one hand and started ticking off fingers with the index finger of her other hand. "If I'm in the human spaces of the station, I only need one guard. If I go into places that aliens have access to, then I need at least two."

"Correct," Peter confirmed, smiling at her. "We're not going to have any issues, are we?"

Anne shook her head. "I hope having security with me will mean I don't have to kill anyone else because they've done something stupid."

Anne could feel Stevie's eyes on her as Peter asked, "How are you holding up?"

"Jinx has suggested that I probably need counseling," Anne admitted. "I've been having some terrible nightmares."

"I guess the million-dollar question is, do you agree with Jinx?" Peter asked, observing Anne.

"Yeah, I do. Look at the mess my mother turned into because of her untreated issues. I really don't want to go there," Anne said with a slight shudder.

"We have a couple people who are trained to handle PTSD. Anyone on your team," Peter once again indicated the guards, "can tell you how to get an appointment when you're ready."

Anne nodded as she replied, "Thanks, it won't be very long. I don't imagine it'll stop the nightmares, but if it helps me get a handle on them I'm more than willing to talk to someone."

"Right now I really need to talk to Stevie, so she can get home before she gets into trouble." Anne looked at the Were who had been introduced as 'Arthur Connors.' "Tell me what I need to know about how the security detail is going to work."

"While you are home," he answered, "there should always be one of us outside your door." He pointed to the door in question.

Jinx chuffed in amusement. "I'm glad you clarified that."

"Doh, I guess that was a little overboard," Arthur admitted. "On school days, one of us will accompany you to and from campus. We'll be stationed in the office while you're in class so we can monitor the school's security cameras. When you need to go into the more public areas, please inform us at least sixty minutes in advance."

"Well, that's going to put a kink in my binge retail therapy." Anne pouted.

"*Gott Verdammt,*" Arthur muttered. "I'm not carrying your bags," he stated emphatically.

Jinx chuffed, then actually howled with amusement.

Arthur looked at Peter, then Jinx, and finally a now-giggling Anne. "What?"

"*Men!*" Stevie said derisively.

"*What?*" Arthur repeated, now looking at the female Were.

She pointed to the couch and coffee table. "She had to drag extra chairs in from the kitchen. What is there about this space that suggests she some sort of shopaholic?"

"Oh, um…" Arthur looked uncomfortable as he held his hands up and shrugged.

Peter stood, and motioned Anne's new security team toward the door. "Why don't we get you people set up while the ladies take care of their business," he said as he followed them. "Talk to you later, Anne. Call me if you have any issues."

"You got it." Anne smiled and waved to the backs of Peter and her Guardian Marine team as they headed into the corridor.

Anne waited until the door closed, then moved to Peter's chair and turned it to face Stevie. "Anything I can get you before we start our discussion?"

Stevie looked somewhat embarrassed as she answered, "I could really use a trip to the bathroom."

"Sure thing. Down the hall, first on the left." Anne pointed her in the right direction. "Can I get you anything while you're taking care of business?" she asked as Stevie stepped past her.

"No, I'm good," Stevie said, shaking her head. "I just hadn't expected to be here this long."

"That makes two of us," Anne admitted.

"Three," Jinx chuffed.

Stevie washed her hands and checked herself in the mirror. She hadn't really needed to use the facilities, but it gave her a few minutes' privacy to get her thoughts in order. Finding out that a prospective employer had been assigned her own security team by the Empress herself had been a shock. Hearing that she had recently killed someone required a few private minutes to digest. While Stevie was somewhat of an anomaly in that she tried to avoid conflict, Weres as a race were a violent people. She had, of course, heard stories as she grew up about Were-on-Were and Were-on-human violence, but none of her acquaintances had done more than get into a few scrapes. Exiting the bathroom, Stevie squared her shoulders and headed for the common room to find out what her future might bring.

"Everything all right?" Anne asked when the Were returned.

"Yep, everything's good," Stevie replied as she resumed her seat. "So, what do you have for me?"

"Unfortunately there's not a whole bunch I can tell you right now. I'm not trying to be difficult, but I'm doing some top-secret work for Bethany Anne." Anne wore a slightly embarrassed look as she admitted this.

"As in an 'if I tell you I'll have to kill you' secret?" Stevie teased.

"Pretty much," Anne said, now looking very serious. "At the least, it's the type of top-secret that requires you to have a pre-employment interview with Ranger One."

Stevie had always been proud of her self-control, but she couldn't stop her eyes from widening at the mention of Barnabas, Bethany Anne's first Ranger. "You're not pulling my leg, are you?"

"Nope. Orders came straight from Bethany Anne herself," Jinx inserted.

"Well, crap. What *can* you tell me?" Despite any apprehension about an interview with Barnabas, Stevie found herself becoming interested, even intrigued.

Anne took a sip of her Coke and idly twisted some of her hair around a finger. "Sorry, but this has to be vague. I was doing some testing and ended up with a totally unexpected result. Now I have the task of attempting to make something workable out of my mistake. The trouble is, I don't have a clue how or where to start. I talked to Jean Dukes, but she is too busy to help me. However, she suggested I talk to the Empress about doing my own R&D, so now I need to find some crazy smart people. I just don't know if crazy is more important than smart in this instance."

Stevie raised a finger in the air as if she were in school and wanting to ask a question.

Anne nodded to her.

"I feel I'm fairly smart and I admit to being a nutcase, but why me?" Stevie gave voice to the question that had been banging around in her head for the last few seconds.

"It was W." Jinx chuffed in amusement. She was proud of her play on words, which originated from a movie she had seen that had some guy called "Q."

"W?" The confusion was evident in Stevie's voice.

Behave yourself! We don't want to give the girl so much of a hard time that we scare her off, Anne warned Jinx. "She's being a smartass," Anne informed Stevie. "She means William from Team BMW. You know those old James Bond movies with the guy called 'Q?'"

"He was the guy who invented all of Double-Oh-Seven's goodies, correct?" Stevie confirmed.

"Yep, that's the guy." Jinx nodded her head in an imitation of human behavior, as she answered. "And, hey, don't blame me for using it. I wasn't the one who came up with 'Team BMW.'"

Stevie looked at the German Shepherd. She had heard all the stories about how intelligent the dogs were, but this was the first time she'd personally experienced it. She glanced at Anne. "She's right." She nodded at the dog. "I can see how it fits."

Anne groaned and put her face in her hands. "Oh God, don't encourage her," she muttered through her fingers, then lifted her head and looked at Stevie. "So that's it, basically. Jean was too busy, and someone suggested that William, or 'W,'" she pointed her finger at Jinx, "might have heard of or know someone who would be able to help us. Bethany Anne had no idea who we'd find. She just insisted that any potential new team members be verified by Barnabas."

Anne watched Stevie's face start to turn red with offended outrage. Anne held up her hand to stop the Were before Stevie even got started. "I'm here today because Bethany Anne rescued me from a booby-trapped bed. My own father was blackmailed to leak secrets from his work." Anne's voice went flat as she delivered the last sentence. "You can see why the Empress might insist that anyone allowed access to sensitive information doesn't have any conflicting loyalties."

Stevie sat quietly for a moment, absorbing the information Anne had just given her. "Barnabas?"

"It's either him or Bethany Anne, and Barnabas is easier to get time with," Anne explained.

"It's just kind of creepy, having him read my mind," Stevie said with a small shudder.

"I don't think you have to worry about him going through your fantasies or anything like that." Anne noticed an interesting blush on Stevie's face. "I imagine he'll just ask you one or two questions that will allow him to pinpoint your loyalties."

Stevie looked relieved. "That makes a certain amount of sense," she admitted. "When do you think I'll be able to see him?"

"Seshat, is Barnabas currently on the station?" Anne asked her EI.

"Meredith says he is in his quarters," Seshat informed her.

"Would you please ask him when he would be available to do a security scan?" Anne requested.

Within several seconds Seshat informed them that, "Barnabas says he is free right now."

Anne noticed Stevie's exaggerated gulp from the corner of her eye. "Would you prefer a different time?"

Stevie shook her head. "Now is fine. Just let me message my parents so they know I will be home late."

"Go for it." Anne gave Stevie a thumbs-up. "Seshat, please ask Barnabas where he wants to meet."

"Barnabas says he is on his way to meet you here," the EI informed her.

"Well, that is convenient." Anne waved to get Stevie's attention. The young Were was talking to her mother, and when she looked up Anne motioned to herself and pointed to the kitchen.

Stevie nodded briefly to Anne to indicate that she understood, then she returned to the conversation with her mother. "Really, Mom, it's a job interview."

"Turn your tablet around so I can see the room," Stevie's mom demanded. After Stevie had complied, her mother scowled. "That doesn't look like a business to me!"

Jinx could hear both sides of Stevie's conversation, and she went over to stick her nose into Stevie's tablet. "That's because it's a new business and we don't have official space yet," Jinx growled to Stevie's mother. Jinx then chuffed her amusement when Stevie's mother moved her tablet to arm's length and her eyes widened in shock.

"Which one are you?" the woman asked.

"I'm Jinx. I'm partnered with Anne," the dog exclaimed proudly.

Realizing that Jinx' entry into the conversation had changed her mother's attitude, Stevie set the tablet on the coffee table so that both she and Jinx were visible. "Anne is currently in the kitchen. I'm guessing she's putting together some sort of snack tray since Ranger One is on his way over." It was excellent timing that just then Anne reappeared from the kitchen carrying a tray with three Cokes, along with some sort of chips and dip. Stevie pointed at her tablet and then motioned for Anne to come into the camera's range. "Mom, meet Anne. Jinx and Anne, this is my mother, Irina Kasyanov."

"Nice to meet you, ma'am," Anne said as she bent to slide her tray of snacks onto the table.

"You truly have work for my *devochka*?" Irina asked.

Anne realized that she'd have to be careful about what she said. "Yes, ma'am. I've known the Empress since before we left Earth, and a few weeks ago she asked me to do some odd jobs for her. I've discovered that to complete some of them, I need someone who can make me some tools. All the adults were too busy with their own work to have time for mine, so I needed to find someone who could help me out. Your daughter came quite highly recommended, so I'm hoping we will well work together."

The woman in the tablet started shaking her finger at her daughter. "You behave, and don't embarrass…"

>>Anne, my exterior camera shows that Guardian Marine Abigail is talking with Barnabas.<<

Stevie noticed that Anne was heading toward the door. "Mom, I'll be on my best behavior, but I have to go right now." She shook her head as her mother kept telling her that she needed to behave and be polite and… "Mom. *MOM!* I have to go, or I'll be talking on my tablet instead of greeting Ranger One." Stevie waited until her mother clicked off before smiling with the satisfaction that she had finally found a way to get her mother to end the call.

CHAPTER TEN

Abby Himmel didn't know why Anne needed a bodyguard, and luckily she didn't *need* to know why to do her job. After being introduced to Anne, she and her cousin E had briefly discussed their rotation with their Were partner Arthur Connors outside the apartment. Abby had drawn first shift, and a quick scan of the environment identified an area with some shadow that still had a clear line of sight to the door. It wasn't dark enough to hide her from a Were or a vampire, but most humans and a lot of aliens would walk right by and never know she was there.

She'd been on duty for almost an hour when she observed a man walking down the hallway toward her. She'd seen the man before, as Barnabas would sometimes visit their workout area to spar with the troops. Abby moved from her corner to take up a position that was in sight of the door. She had noticed a camera over the door earlier, and her new location would ensure she was visible to whoever was monitoring the camera feed. Watching the vampire approach Abigail was once again fascinated by the man's movement. Barnabas' gait was pure economy of motion; the man had turned walking into an art form.

Barnabas approached the address that Meredith had told him was the residence of the young woman Anne. He slowed slightly at the sight of a woman standing outside the door, but a quick mental scan identified her as a Guardian Marine. Barnabas was curious. She wore a light jacket, but didn't seem to be armed.

He stopped just a few feet in front of Abigail. "Good evening, Marine Himmel. Is this a weapons-free zone?" he asked, then added with a slight smile, "If a person spends several hundred years walking everywhere they go... Well, let's just say that practice makes perfect."

In her own form of "practice makes perfect," Abby's hand twitched from where it had been resting at her hip and produced an Uzi. "No, sir, not weapons-free, although this isn't my favorite at the ranges we're talking about here." Abby tilted her head toward the hall behind Barnabas. "This should make a real mess of anything not wearing armor."

Barnabas eyed the weapon in the Marine's hand with interest. "Uzi?"

Abigail inclined her head. "Uzi Pro, to be exact. This was the latest iteration when we left Earth." She extended the folding forearm brace, displaying the weapon to Barnabas. "It can empty a thirty-round magazine in under two seconds, and the forearm brace provides excellent one-handed control. At these short ranges, the nine-millimeter cartridge is reasonably effective on soft targets."

Abby strongly suspected that even thirty rounds in two seconds would only piss the old vampire off. With that in mind, she folded the forearm brace back against the body of the weapon and slid it back behind her. "May I see some identification, please sir?" Abigail asked in her politest voice.

Barnabas smiled and tapped his temple as he watched the Marine conceal her submachine gun. "I think you're right. I'd probably survive it if you shot me, but I imagine it would hurt like crazy. And ID? You already know who I am."

"That may be, sir, but I don't have any Jedi mind tricks, so it is in my job to ask for identification," Abigail stated firmly.

Barnabas chuckled as he pulled the old-fashioned leather case from a pocket and displayed his Ranger One badge. He approved of the dedication the Marine was displaying. "Is this sufficient?"

"Absolutely, sir. You're here to see Anne?" Abigail remained formal.

"I am, and if you knock and announce me quickly, said young lady won't open the door on her own initiative. This way I can explain the proper protocol, which will save you from having to inform her that she has broken a rule she doesn't even know about." Barnabas waved a hand toward the door to hurry Abigail along.

Abby turned and knocked on the door—which opened instantly, thus proving the old vampire's point. "Ranger One is here to see you, ma'am."

Anne looked at the bodyguard. She hadn't even known someone was out there until Seshat had told her she was talking to Barnabas. "Ma'am?" Anne couldn't stop her eyes from widening as she asked.

"I could do 'Miss' if you'd prefer," Abby offered.

Anne nodded vigorously. "When you use 'ma'am' I expect see my mother."

"Very well, Miss." Abby's training allowed her to maintain a straight face. "Ranger One is here to see you."

Anne stepped back to clear the door and motioned for Barnabas to enter. She was about to stick her head back outside to ask the Marine if she wanted anything when Barnabas put a hand on her arm and shook his head.

Once the door closed Barnabas greeted Jinx, and noticing the tray of refreshments, he sat down and plucked a few chips from the bowl. Once he had eaten a couple chips he looked up at Anne, who was still standing. "I know you are new to having a security detail, so what I am about to say is not a criticism. It's just information. Two things: first, don't open the door until your guard notifies you of a visitor." Barnabas could tell from her expression that Anne wanted to say something, and instead of reading her mind he looked at her and asked, "You have an issue with that?"

Anne looked slightly confused. "Seshat had already informed me you were here."

Barnabas cut in before Anne could continue. "That may be, but your guard doesn't know that, and having a door open behind him is a distraction he doesn't need. The second thing is—and I know you are trying to be polite—while they are on duty, don't offer refreshments or the like."

"Another distraction?"

"Exactly," Barnabas confirmed. "You would be boxing them in, so to speak. They wouldn't want to upset you by refusing, but to do their jobs correctly they need their hands free."

"Ok, that makes sense." Anne smiled. "Thanks, I appreciate you letting me know."

Barnabas grabbed a few more chips and stood. "Then my work here is done."

Anne looked flustered and started to sputter. "But… but…" She pointed at Stevie.

"She's approved. Go ahead and hire her for whatever you need her to do," Barnabas declared, then looked at Stevie. "Just promise me you will inform one of us if someone tries to threaten or blackmail you."

Stevie just sat there with a shocked expression on her face, then nodded vigorously. "Yes, sir. Absolutely, sir!"

"Excellent." Barnabas held a chip in front of his mouth. "I expect I'll be seeing more of you, then," he said, crunching down on the chip as he let himself out of the apartment.

* * *

Stevie gave a brief nod to the Marine as she left Anne's apartment to head home. She didn't know whether she was shell-shocked, or gobsmacked, but it seemed like her head was spinning. Just this morning she had been a normal student. Well, except for shop, where she was freaking astounding. Too bad Old Man Jerk-ins had to be such a bistok butt. She had never seen a bistok, but everything she had ever heard indicated that if you looked up "Nasty-ass gross" in the dictionary there'd be a picture of a bistok.

Stevie made sure to monitor her surroundings with

SR RUSSELL & MICHAEL ANDERLE

extra care on her way home. She wasn't exactly certain why her new boss had a Guardian Marine team for security, but she wasn't going to risk being caught unaware if it had something to do with this new project.

Project! What a way to term what she had been shown after Barnabas left. Seshat had played a couple videos of Anne's first tests, then Anne had burnt another hole in her coffee table giving a live demonstration.

Stevie pushed some loose hair behind her ear. When Anne said she wanted to weaponize her experiment, Stevie had barely managed to refrain from shaking her head. How were they going to turn something that could burn through rock into a weapon? Stevie growled under her breath. That sort of thinking was only going to result in failure. The question she should be asking was, what steps did they need to take to create a weapon that could burn through rock.

Stevie was very pleased to find that her mother had kept a plate of supper warm for her. Weres burned lots of energy and needed a lot of calories. The little snacks that Anne had set out were the type a person saw at a social event, not to satisfy a hungry stomach.

Stevie was bemused by the contradiction. Anne didn't seem to be the sort of person who attended social events, so it made her wonder where Anne had learned that type of entertaining. Another memory nagged at Stevie as she sat down to her dinner, and her eyes widened as the memory surfaced. Peter had talked to Anne like she had killed someone. Stevie decided she should probably ignore that subject. Asking possibly offensive questions might be detrimental to her health. What was that ancient Chinese curse?

Oh yeah. "May you live in interesting times."

It sure had been a busy evening. Anne was cleaning up the extra dishes she had used while entertaining her unexpected guests when Seshat spoke.

>>You have a comm message from a Mr. Frank Kurns. <<

Wait, how did he know to call you?

>>He didn't call me, he called your tablet. Since you were busy, I diverted the message. I can display it on my main screen when you're ready.<<

I am not upset with you, but just for your information, normal procedure would have been to ask the person first if they were all right with you doing that, Anne explained to her newborn EI.

>> I apologize. It just seemed the most efficient way to do things.<<

It probably is. Just refer to my comment about biologicals.

>>Oh! I'll remember to ask permission next time.<<

"Is Frank still on the line, or did he just leave a message?" Anne asked as she reentered the common room.

"He's waiting." Seshat copied Anne and spoke aloud.

"Okay," Anne said as she took a seat on the couch and looked at the screen that was displaying Seshat's avatar. "Accept the call, please."

The screen on the wall now hosted two frames. Seshat's

avatar was in one, and a middle-aged man inhabited the other.

"Good evening, young lady. My name is Frank Kurns. Bethany Anne claims you are the angel who is going to save me from the incredible boredom I have been suffering," the man stated theatrically.

Anne couldn't restrain her giggle. "I find it hard to believe Bethany Anne called me an angel."

The man looked smug. "I was raised in a much more genteel time. I may have translated Bethany Anne's words to better suit my delicate sensibilities."

Anne was shocked, first that the man could talk this way, and second that he could say that with a straight face. "I'll just take your word for that."

"Flowery language aside, Bethany Anne told me you might need someone with organizational skills," Frank stated with an eager gleam in his eyes.

"I have a Guardian Marines security team and one employee already, with possibly more in the future. I'm still in school, and I'm not studying business. I don't have a clue how to hire, pay, offer benefits…" Anne sputtered to a stop and shook her head, the scope of the project in front of her daunting.

Frank nodded confidently. "That's what I'm here to do. Eventually Bethany Anne may have other work she will need me for, but right now I have the time to be like your CEO and get you started. If the Empress needs me to handle something else, I'll make sure she gives me time to find and hire a replacement. You won't be left high and dry."

"Will you think less of me if I admit how wonderful that sounds?" Anne asked.

"Not at all! I wasn't kidding with the 'saving me from boredom' comment. Bethany Anne has ADAM to handle the sort of tasks I used to be responsible for. I'll admit that I had been thinking of retiring back on Earth, but a lot of that was just my old bones not handling the cold and damp as well as they used to."

Anne carefully studied the man on the screen. "I take it you have benefited from some of the nanotech Bethany Anne controls?"

"I applaud your deductive capabilities," Frank said, clapping his hands quietly.

"Do I need to do anything to get this up and running?"

Frank shook his head. "No, Bethany Anne provided enough details to get me started. You and I will need to meet in person one day soon so that you can bring me up-to-date on what you will need and I can explain what you need to know."

"That sounds great," Anne stated enthusiastically. "Seshat knows my schedule, so you can contact her when you're ready to get together."

Frank's smile made him look extremely happy. "That sounds like a plan, and as they use to say on this silly show I used to watch, 'I love it when a plan comes together.' I'll contact your EI in the next few days."

Anne shook her head violently. "You'll contact Seshat," she corrected emphatically.

Frank Kurns might not look his age anymore, but he had been around for a lot of years. His experience made it quite easy to recognize that he had put his foot in it. "My apologies. I will contact *Seshat* within the next few days to set up a meeting with you." He smiled again to reassure the young woman who was looking at him with steely eyes that he had not been offended.

Anne's expression softened as she nodded in agreement. "I will talk to you later, then."

With the immediate business concluded, Anne wished Frank a good evening, signed off, and headed to bed. While she still expected the nightmares, she was relieved to know that she wasn't going to have to fumble around on her own to get her research group going.

CHAPTER ELEVEN

The days that followed fell into a pattern: school, home-work, and then to the apartment to do testing. One of Stevie's first contributions was a test stand, which was five feet tall and had grooves at the top they could slide tiles into. Stevie had found a formula for silica ceramics, and Cheryl Lynn had directed them to a small company that could produce about twenty-five tiles a week. At the base of the stand was a two-foot-deep water tank. Water wouldn't stop a ruby that was still being powered from the Etheric, but if Anne cut the power before it hit the water, the ruby cooled enough to not cause any damage by the time it sank to the bottom. Each evening Stevie and Anne placed the ruby beside other samples, trying to find a material that the ruby wouldn't vaporize.

"Guardian Connors just commed to let you know that Bethany Anne and Ashur are outside," Seshat's avatar informed them.

Anne was unwrapping a new sample while Stevie replaced the top two tiles, and she put the heavily perforated tiles into the crate they were using for trash. Stevie smiled as she watched Anne head for the door.

They were not any closer to finding a solution, but even so, Stevie felt a sense of accomplishment. When they had first started using the tiles, the ruby would burn through four of them before Anne could stop it. Day by day Anne was exhibiting more control; now she only burned through two. She was proud of her friend's progress. Friend? Stevie pondered that as she listened to Anne enthusiastically welcome Ashur. *Yes*, she thought, *I have a friend*. She hugged herself briefly, enjoying the new feeling, and turned to greet the Empress.

Bethany Anne reached down to rub Jinx' ears as she watched Anne hug Ashur. As she stepped into the apartment and saw Stevie, she couldn't help but chuckle at TOM's comment.

For a Were, she looks as pale as those vampires in the old movies from Earth.

Funny, I hadn't made that connection, but you're correct.

"If you bow, kneel, curtsy, or any other such nonsense, I'll kick you so hard that Anne won't find you until Monday!" Bethany Anne pointedly informed the young Were. She suspected that it was only the fear of doing it wrong that had prevented the girl from some sort of obeisance. "As I'm sure you already know, I'm Bethany Anne." She held out her hand.

"Oh gosh, I'm so sorry," Anne exclaimed as she rushed to Bethany Anne's side. "I got so caught up with saying hello to Ashur that I forgot my manners. Bethany Anne, this is Stephanie Kasyanov, although she prefers to be called Stevie. Stevie, this is Ashur's person, Bethany Anne."

Ashur chuffed in amused agreement as his wagging tail thumped against the couch.

As Bethany Anne shook the Were's hand, she looked at Anne. "That was nicely done. Keep that up, and I'll make you an ambassador."

Anne shrugged. "I know how tired you get of all the royalty stuff you have to put up with. I just tried to find a way to introduce you without any of that crap."

"I take it you're not interested in an ambassadorial position?" Bethany Anne teased.

"No thanks. Being a researcher… Oh, can I get you a Coke? And to finish answering your question, being a researcher is tough enough, thanks," Anne said with complete sincerity.

Bethany Anne flopped down on the couch, and when Ashur lay on the floor in front of her, she stretched out her legs to rest her calves on his rump. "I can't remember the last time I turned down a Coke," she said as she tilted her head back and thought. She shook her head briefly. "Nope, can't remember, so yes. A Coke would be wonderful. Thanks."

"Stevie?" Anne asked as she headed for the kitchen.

Stevie looked at her half-full bottle on the coffee table. "I'm good for now, thanks."

Anne returned from the kitchen carrying two Cokes in one hand and a dinette chair in the other. She offered the chair to Stevie, and flopped down on the opposite end of the couch. "Here you go." She offered one of the cold bottles to Bethany Anne, and opened her own. After taking two swallows that were large enough to cause her mother to chide her for unfeminine behavior, she set the bottle on the floor and looked at Bethany Anne. "What can we do for you?"

Bethany Anne opened her Coke and took several sips before answering. "Thanks, I needed that!" She looked at one girl and then the other. "Something was flagged to my attention the other day about how none of the samples you've been requisitioning are getting returned anymore. I was rapidly losing patience listening to ambassadors and trade representatives whine about why they should get preferential treatment, so claiming I had something else I needed to look into got me away before I went all 'Queen Bitch' on them."

"Um, I hope you left the need to go all 'Queen Bitch' back there," Stevie commented nervously.

Bethany Anne reached for her Coke again and took a couple more sips. "Yeah," she said finally, and sighed with contentment. "It would require a monumental fuckup for the Queen Bitch to show up here. That doesn't stop me from wondering what's happening to the samples, however."

"Do you wish a live demonstration, or do you just want Seshat to fast-forward through hours of video?" Anne's face was tight as she queried Bethany Anne.

It was like Bethany Anne had just explained to the girls. She'd been having a bad day playing Empress. Her relief at escaping the bistok-shit bureaucrats and arriving some-place where she could just be herself had blinded her temporarily to the conditions of the room. It was a mess! Most of the furniture had been pushed into one corner, while the other end of the room held what looked like a dinette table, a tall contraption with a tank of water at its base, and several open crates.

"Let's go for the live demo, and have Seshat send ADAM copies of those videos," Bethany Anne suggested.

Anne jumped up and resumed opening the sample that Bethany Anne's arrival had interrupted.

Stevie got up and, swallowing her nervousness, started explaining to Bethany Anne how their test tower worked while she added two new tiles. She motioned for Bethany Anne to come over, then took their ruby and the sample Anne had just unwrapped and set them side-by-side on the top tile.

"We're trying to find a substance the energized ruby can't destroy, but so far we haven't had any luck," Stevie explained, then asked, "You recording this, Seshat?"

The very pretty girl who was Seshat's avatar crossed her arms on the monitor. "Certainly. I've been instructed to record all testing."

Bethany Anne noted the acerbic tone of the avatar's reply. *ADAM?*

>>She's coming along quite nicely, don't you think?<<
You built Anne an AI?

>>Not exactly. Are you sure you want to have this discussion now?<<

Probably not, but we will *talk about it.*

Bethany Anne watched as Anne powered the ruby. It flared to life, destroying the second sample while burning through the tile it rested on and the one below that.

"And that," Anne sighed with disgust, "sums up our present progress."

"Have you tried it against another ruby?" Bethany Anne

inquired, then had to bite the inside of her lip to keep from smiling when both teen girls rolled their eyes.

"Seshat, would you please play the footage of the two-ruby test?" Anne requested politely.

Bethany Anne watched almost identical copy of the experiment that had just been performed in front of her. The only difference was that the active ruby had burned through four tiles before it had died out.

Bethany Anne?

What you got, TOM?

Has she tried powering both rubies at the same time?

Bethany Anne rubbed the back of her neck. *I'll ask.* "Have you tried powering two rubies at once?"

Watching the girls was amusing. Stevie muttered, "Oh, fuck!" and Anne grabbed two handfuls of hair, crying, "How could I be so stupid?"

"If it helps at all, TOM came up with the suggestion," Bethany Anne confessed.

"Even so," Stevie proclaimed, "it's so basic it should have been the first thing I thought of."

Anne pulled another ruby out of the samples crate. "How do we work this?"

Stevie took the rubies and set them on opposite edges of the tile stack. "First let's see if you can power them both at the same time."

After fifteen minutes of watching Anne fail to ignite the two gems simultaneously, Bethany Anne interrupted. "Why don't you teach me how to power one? Then we could try powering one each."

Thirty minutes later Bethany Anne had a headache, but that didn't stop her from jumping to her feet and pumping her fist when she was successful. "Okay, now how do we make this work?"

Stevie started stacking tiles on the table in two overlapping columns that met at the bottom. "I've been thinking about that while you two have been practicing. I'm hoping that as a gem burns through a tile, it will shift toward the center when it hits the angled tile below it. If each of you can keep your ruby burning at a steady rate, the fields should meet right about here." Stevie pointed to a spot about three inches from the bottom of her structure. "What happens then is anyone's guess."

Anne and Bethany Anne spent another hour fine-tuning their control in an attempt to synchronize their efforts, but finally Anne wiped away a tear. "If we're going to try this, we need to do it now. I'm toast."

Bethany Anne, who was experiencing a nasty headache herself, nodded carefully in agreement. "Let me splash some water on my face while Stevie is setting up, and we'll give it the old college try."

She noticed a confused look on Stevie's face as she headed for the bathroom and heard Anne say, "It's old-people talk. My dad uses several of those." Bethany Anne was certain the extra buzzing in her head was TOM trying his hardest not to burst out laughing.

After they had all visited the bathroom, Bethany Anne sat beside Anne and they focused on Stevie's V-shaped construct.

CHAPTER TWELVE

Arthur Connors had been very pleased when his team had been offered the bodyguard job. He hadn't been told what the young lady was doing to make her a possible target, but his briefing had indicated that both she and the dog Jinx could be abduction targets. Having the Empress herself show up for a meeting with the girls in the apartment had been a surprise. Whatever they were doing was obviously way above his pay grade.

He and his Marines had set up a six-hour shift rotation. One of them was always with the girl while a second was on standby. The second could grab a bite or just kick back and relax, but they had to be ready to respond if the situation required a two-person team. The third team member's job was to sleep. As he stood guard, Arthur clenched and released muscles in his legs and arms to keep them loose without moving around enough to attract attention. He had just put his hands on the small of his back to stretch it when movement caught his eye.

"TOM says that Bethany Anne had started to wonder if she could get away with stuffing a few of the bureaucrats into the Etheric," Matrix said, to explain why he and John were walking to Jinx' place. "Instead of following through with the idea, she claimed she had an appointment and headed here to talk to Jinx and her person." Both John and Matrix noticed the Guardian as they approached the target apartment.

John offered his hand as the Guardian stepped from the shadows. "Connors, right?"

"Arthur Connors. We've only met during training. It will be nice to shake your hand without getting tossed across the room," he stated.

"Ready?" the Were asked the two vampires.

"Born that way," Bethany Anne responded at the same moment Anne muttered, "As I'll ever be."

"Three, two, one, *now*!"

Their practice paid off. There wasn't even a half-second's difference in the two gems flaring to life. Stevie clenched her fists. It was working! When the rubies burnt through a level and dropped onto the sloped tile underneath, they shifted toward the center slightly before burning the next hole in a downward vertical path.

No one could have predicted what happened next. For the first time since they'd started experimenting, one ruby moved instead of burning into the substance it struck—Anne's ruby bounced sideways toward Bethany Anne's.

Bethany Anne didn't even blink; she didn't have enough time. She wasn't sure what was going to occur when the energy fields generated by the rubies met, but she didn't want to be in the same room.

Bethany Anne switched into her fastest vampire speed as she heard TOM mutter, **I've got a bad feeling about this.** A quick glance told her that Anne had her arm around Jinx' neck.

Ashur felt his person's emotions spike with desperation. Apparently they all needed to get out of here *fast*. He grabbed the female Were's wrist in his jaws and pointed his tail toward his person.

Bethany Anne wasn't going to place bets on whether they'd make it out alive, but seeing Ashur move toward Stevie gave her hope. She grabbed Anne, then wanted to laugh when she turned back to find Ashur's tail within reach. Hoping Ashur had a good grip on Stevie, Bethany Anne moved them all into the Etheric.

Guardian Connors was being entertained by the stories John was telling him about the early days with Bethany Anne. Arthur had never fought the Forsaken, and he found himself surprised and impressed that four guys who had been baseline human in those days had survived the experience. John had just started to tell him about a situation Bethany Anne had dealt with in Las Vegas when an explosion in the apartment refocused everyone's attention.

Stevie looked around at the gray nowhere place she found herself. She had been watching the test, and then Ashur had bitten down on her wrist and suddenly she was *here*. Stevie was glad to see Bethany Anne, Jinx, and Anne with her and Ashur.

Sorry. Ashur whined as he let go of the Were. *No time to be gentle.*

"It's okay." Stevie pulled up her sleeve to show Ashur that he hadn't broken skin. "Just a couple of bruises that will clear up in minutes."

"Everyone all right?" Bethany Anne asked as she checked her three passengers for damage.

"Wow, cool! We're in the Etheric, but what happened?" Anne wondered as she looked Jinx over to ensure her friend was safe.

"No damage here, just not quite sure what happened," Stevie informed Bethany Anne.

Once Bethany Anne had confirmed to her own satisfaction that no one was hurt, she looked at the Were. "As Anne observed, we're in the Etheric. I'm not clairvoyant, but I suddenly felt it wasn't a good idea to be in the same room when those fields met. Thankfully, with Ashur's help," she knelt and hugged her longtime companion, "everyone was close enough to grab, so we made a hasty exit."

"What do we do now?" Anne wanted to know.

"Hang on a sec," Bethany Anne said, then stuck her head back into the station to make sure it was safe to step into the hallway outside Anne's apartment. Guardian Connors was pounding frantically on the door and demanding entry. John and Matrix were standing behind the Were, but weren't panicking yet.

>>**John is asking if you are all right.**<< ADAM informed her.

Are you handling that? Bethany Anne asked hopefully.

>>**I haven't told him anything yet, but I will bring him up to date.**<<

Returning to the Etheric, she took hold of Ashur. *Thanks, ADAM.* She held out her other arm, telling the girls to grab on tightly. Making sure Anne had a good grip on Jinx, Bethany Anne moved them all back to the *Meredith Reynolds*.

I told you... Ashur started to say.

Bethany Anne sighed and admitted, *Yes, you did tell me.* She reached down and gave the spot behind Ashur's head a good scratch. Dogs, whether they were Kurtherian-enhanced or not, had a hard time scratching that spot themselves.

"I suppose you ratted me out?" she asked Matrix.

"Nope, no rats involved. I'm *dogging* your steps," Matrix snarked as he checked his sister.

"Oh, jeez! That stinks worse than wet dog." Bethany Anne couldn't hide her smile. "Evening, Mr. Grimes." Bethany Anne batted her lashes at John.

John managed to refrain from smiling. He just shook his head at Bethany Anne, doing his best to look disapproving and disappointed at the same time.

Seshat, would you open the door please? Anne requested.

>>I've sent the signal to the door, but it's returning an error message. The explosion destroyed my camera, so I no longer have video of the interior of the apartment.<<

Explosion?

>>I reviewed the video. There were several changes as the rubies got closer to each other, but at a distance of zero-point-one-three millimeters they exploded.<<

"Seshat says there was an explosion and her commands to open the door are returning an error message," Anne informed the small group outside the apartment.

"Can she see if it's blocked, or…" Bethany Anne's query came to a halt when Anne shook her head.

"It appears the camera we devoted to Seshat's use is no longer functioning."

Bethany Anne thought for a few seconds, and made a decision. "Hold on, I'll be right back." She spoke for the benefit of the group, but looked at John.

Bethany Anne stepped into the Etheric, then moved carefully to where she thought Anne's kitchen should be. She cautiously stuck her head into real space, and found she had guessed correctly. Given that the door was not responding Bethany Anne had expected some damage to the interior, but what she observed shocked even her. There was a small hole right through the wall between the kitchen and common area. Peeking into the common room, she found the whole area slagged. It was obvious why the door wouldn't open: the rock of the interior surface of that wall had fused.

Bethany Anne stepped through the Etheric to her own apartment and entered her weapons room. She picked up the hilt of her Etheric sword, then went back into the realm. After taking a quick peek at the hall in front of Anne's apartment, she emerged behind the group who were loitering around the doorway.

"Make a hole, people," Bethany Anne commanded as she walked toward the door. Once she had a clear space, she energized her Etheric sword and cut all the way around the door. After deactivating the blade, she secured the hilt to her belt. As she turned to face the group, she mentally catalogued its makeup. Two vampires, including herself, two Weres, a heavily modified human, and three modified canines. While the dogs were impressive, none were suitable for the task at hand. Any of the humanoids were probably strong enough to move the door. *To hell with it*, she thought, and smiled at John. *I don't have to live with the others.*

"Mr. Grimes, would you be so kind as to open the door?" Bethany Anne asked with a smile.

"Laying it on a little thick, aren't you BA?" John asked as Bethany Anne moved aside to allow him access.

Bethany Anne glanced at the two young women, who were now giggling at the byplay between her and John. Then she looked at John and batted her eyelashes again, saying, "Why Mr. Grimes, I have *nooo* idea what you're talking about."

"Riigghhhttt." John drew out the word as he teased back. Knowing that Bethany Anne was perfectly capable of moving the door herself, he was pleased that she had asked him to do it. John turned and put his back to the door, then crouched a little so he applied force to the middle area. He started exerting pressure, and was surprised at just how easily the door moved. Once he had pushed it inward several inches he straightened, turned, and put his hands on the edges. With that grip he simply picked it up and set it out of the way.

John returned to the doorway, and after several theatrical flourishes with his arm he bowed to Bethany Anne. "Your way is open, my Empress." John stood clear of the doorway and gazed into the room. "Holy shi... shkabob," he said, looking over his shoulder at the two teenage girls following Bethany Anne.

Anne reached up and patted John on the chest as she followed Bethany Anne into the room. "In today's times neither our age nor our gender protects us from profanity. Stevie and I have both heard and said worse." Anne turned from John and got a good look. "Holy shit!" she exclaimed. "What the hell happened?"

Bethany Anne had seen some damage from the kitchen, but she slowly looked around Ground Zero. "Not one hundred percent sure, but this is going to play hell with your damage deposit." Bethany Anne teased, then bit her tongue to refrain from smiling at Anne's shocked expression.

>>I have reviewed the footage. While I don't have enough data to explain why it happened, I can describe the event.<<

"Seshat has video up until the time her camera was destroyed," Anne informed Stevie and Bethany Anne. "She's prepared to summarize what occurred, but she doesn't have enough data to determine *why* it happened. Unfortunately," Anne continued as she motioned to the spot on the wall where Seshat's monitor used to be, "we don't have the capability to run the video."

"The video can wait," Bethany Anne informed the girl, then started to pace. "We need to find you new accommodations. For tonight, why don't you crash at Tabitha's?

She's on assignment right now, but she had to leave Dio behind. He'd probably welcome the company."

Bethany Anne continued pacing. "I'll have ADAM contact Marcus and William and see when they can be available for a meeting. He'll inform Seshat once we set a time, then we can all sit down and go through the video."

Bethany Anne stopped and looked at Anne. "I'm as much to blame for this situation as you are, but we got off lucky this time. If the reaction had been a hundred times worse, we might have killed people or damaged the *Meredith Reynolds.*"

Bethany Anne put a hand on the girl's shoulder. "Despite the risk involved, I'm impressed with your discovery, and I look forward to seeing what you finally develop. But—and this is a *big* but—we are going to have to find you a safe workspace. I can't risk the lives of the people on the station if you end up making a bigger bang."

Anne looked at her Empress, then nodded twice. "What should we do for workspace, then?"

How about a small asteroid? TOM suggested. **Find something with the right composition and move it to within the defensive perimeter of the *Meredith Reynolds*, or give it enough weaponry to defend itself until assistance can arrive.**

Both good ideas, but I should probably talk this over with the general and the admiral before making a final decision.

"I think our best solution would be to find a small asteroid we could turn into lab space for you." Bethany Anne looked from Anne to Stevie. "Not that I want to lose either of you, but if you accidentally create a giant explosion it needs to happen somewhere other than here."

"I could probably do the tes—" Anne started.

Stevie quickly cut Anne off. "Not on your life!" She looked down at Jinx. "I don't imagine Jinx will accept being left behind, and I won't either."

Jinx moved to stand by the Were and looked up at her person. "What she said!"

Anne looked at the older vampire. "A little help here?"

Bethany Anne shook her head, and slowly pivoted in place to look around the room. Then she looked at Stevie and Jinx. "You know and understand the risks, right?"

Canine and Were looked at Bethany Anne and nodded.

"They're part of *your* team." Bethany Anne emphasized "your." "Except for the 'no experiments on *Meredith Reynolds*' edict, I have no intention of telling your friends and coworkers what to do. Besides, while I don't remember who first said it, in this instance I'm fairly certain that I should stick to 'Don't give an order you know won't be obeyed.'"

Jinx looked up at Stevie, then sat and held up her front paw for a high-five. Stevie obliged by squatting and tapping Jinx' paw with the palm of her hand. They both looked at Bethany Anne and nodded, confirming that they would ignore any order to not accompany her Etheric Researcher.

Bethany Anne clapped her hands. "All right, then." She looked at John. "Would you please arrange for a guard on the door so that Anne doesn't have to worry about her stuff?"

"Sure thing," John said, and stepped outside the apartment to take care of it.

"Gather what you and Jinx will need for the next couple days," Bethany Anne suggested to Anne.

It only took a few minutes for Anne to pack a couple of bags. Ashur reveled in the goodbye hug he got from Anne. Bethany Anne wasn't typically a huggy person, but she accepted one from Anne.

Stevie offered her own goodbyes to everyone, then headed to her family's home as Anne and Jinx left for Tabitha's under the watchful eye of Arthur Connors.

CHAPTER THIRTEEN

John sighed, took one more look at the destroyed apartment, and grasped Bethany Anne's arm. "Come on, BA, let's get you home."

Bethany Anne patted the back of John's hand. "I need a bit of quiet time, so we'll head home the old-fashioned way."

John checked that his Jean Dukes would sit well while he walked and raised an eyebrow. *You really all right?*

Bethany Anne tapped her temple and smiled briefly. *Yup, just need to have a conversation with my tenants.*

John smiled in return and wiggled his fingers at Bethany Anne. *Sounds good. I'll follow you.*

It was a testament to how close Bethany Anne was to her Bitches that they could have that kind of silent conversation. Ashur and Matrix led as Empress Bethany Anne walked toward her residence, completely confident that John Grimes had her back.

What's up with Anne's computer? she asked ADAM as they strode toward home.

>>Since TOM financed the best hardware available, I decided to provide Anne with the best computer support possible. I didn't create an AI outright, but I made sure the potential was there. I don't mean to be insulting, but if I gave your father the same hardware/software combination he would never produce an AI.<<

Bethany Anne walked quietly for a few seconds, analyzing what ADAM had said. *The general would just consider it a fancy computer. A mere piece of equipment.*

>>That agrees with my assessment. Your father is old-fashioned enough that it would never occur to him to see it as anything other than the latest-generation computer.<<

ADAM paused momentarily, then continued. >>Anne treats people well, and she treats entities as people in the same way you treated me as an individual. I believe that being treated like a person is accelerating the process for Seshat. I wouldn't be surprised to find out that Anne asks Seshat how her day was, or has some similar interaction.<<

That would encourage Seshat to think in the first person.

>>Exactly.<<

While Dio was upset his person had left him behind *again*, he was very pleased to have Anne and Jinx for company. Sensing that her brother was somewhat depressed, the next morning Jinx asked Anne if it was all right to skip school that day.

"Sure, but if you two are going anywhere, we need to ask our security how they want to handle it."

When she opened the door, Anne found E on guard. "I need to head to school, but Jinx and Dio want to hang out together today. How do we handle that?"

"It's my turn to accompany you to school," E stated. "I'll call one of the others to cover Jinx and Dio."

"Would you ask Guardian Connors?" Jinx requested. "He could shift, and we'd all look kind of the same."

Dio chuffed his amusement, then barked in agreement.

When he arrived, Connors was somewhat hesitant to agree to Jinx' plan. "I won't have any comm gear to call for help if I'm in wolf form."

"Not a problem," Jinx countered. "I'm in constant contact with Seshat, so we would just let her know who to contact if we needed assistance."

Since Guardian Connors secretly thought that three canines trotting abreast through the halls would be kind of cool, he agreed to Jinx' plan. Once he was confident of Seshat's ability to contact Abigail, he and the two German Shepherds waited for E and Anne to head out.

Once the women had gone, Arthur stripped and shifted into his wolf form. He wouldn't have hesitated to shift in front of Abigail or E, but he felt a little uncomfortable at the idea of stripping in front of a teenage girl.

Jinx and Dio persuaded Arthur to head to one of the

parks for a game of tag. They spent the next hour burning off a lot of pent-up energy, with the side benefit of entertaining the humans who were visiting the park. Finally tired and somewhat overheated, the three of them called a halt to their game.

"Hey, why don't we go get some ice cream?" Jinx suggested.

"How are we going to pay for it?" Dio wanted to know.

"Umm, I'll have Seshat ask Anne if she'll let her make the payment." Seconds later Jinx told the other two, "Seshat says Anne's agreed to the plan, but I have to tell you to make sure I'm not panting before we order."

"Why's that?" Arthur barked.

Jinx' ears flattened.

"You still get sick if you eat while you're hot?" Dio asked his sister.

"Yes." Jinx whined. "I've tried it a few times since I've been with Anne, and I still get sick every time."

"If we just walk you should be cool by then," Arthur offered after making a calculation in his head.

Dio rolled to his feet. "Let's go," he said eagerly. "Tabitha isn't very good about sharing her ice cream."

"Does Tabitha see you as a dog or as a guy?" Arthur asked Dio.

Dio thought about the question for several seconds. "I don't know, why?"

"It's been my experience that if a female is self-medicating with ice cream, she'll often share with another woman or her pet but rarely with a guy," the Were explained.

"I'm not sure," Dio admitted. "I'll have to... Hey, what's

that noise?" He stopped, ears fully erect, trying to locate the noise he had heard.

"This way." Connors had identified the direction of the sound and turned down a side tunnel.

At the next intersection, Jinx heard a panicked female voice coming from the left passageway. She spun and darted that way, and had only traveled a few yards before the tunnel opened onto a construction site. Jinx stopped so abruptly at the scene in front of her that Dio ran into her rear end. Somehow a plank had been left partially extended over an open pit, and a toddler had managed to crawl along the plank and was now over the pit, crying. A woman—Jinx imagined it must be the mother—was screaming, "Get back here, Joey!"

Jinx grabbed the woman by the back of her blouse and pulled her away from the plank. "Hold her," Jinx told her brother.

Leaving Dio and the Were to deal with the woman, Jinx dropped to her belly and crawled to the edge of the pit. Watching the little boy, she rolled onto her back and stuck all her feet in the air. He stopped crying and peered at Jinx intently. She rolled upright and stuck her rear end in the air, wagging her tail vigorously. Remembering that a human this young would not have an implant and therefore would only hear dog noises, she tried to stick with happy sounds. She yipped softly and spun like she was chasing her tail, then stopped and dropped to her belly.

Score, Jinx thought as the toddler giggled in response to her actions. Jinx shuffled back a few inches and yipped at the boy again. *Come pet the doggy*, she thought as she put her nose between her paws and wagged her tail again. The boy reached toward Jinx, so she rolled onto her side and waved a paw. Then she got back to her feet and spun in another circle. She moved a little bit farther away before she laid back down, then reached out a paw and yipped again. The little boy the woman had called "Joey" smiled and made a happy burbling sound, then started to crawl toward Jinx.

Jinx flopped onto her side again and waved her paws at the boy to encourage him to keep crawling to her. It took several seconds, but eventually little Joey crawled to her neck. Jinx heard Dio growl; she imagined he was keeping the woman under control. Jinx carefully gripped Joey's diaper with her teeth and moved backward, dragging him away from the pit. Joey laughed and clapped his hands as he was lifted off the ground. She turned and held the boy out to the woman, who had sunk to her knees. The lady took the boy, and hugged him tightly as tears streamed down her face.

"What the hell were you doing?" Guardian Connors was in human form, crouching behind Dio to cover his nudity.

The woman blushed. "I just stepped into the passageway to take a call from my boyfriend. I swear I only set Joey down for a second to dig out my tablet."

"As you just found out, it only *takes* a second," Arthur told her.

CHAPTER FOURTEEN

"Why does it seem like Anne and I run into all the weirdos?" Jinx wondered as she licked up the rest of her ice cream.

"What do you mean?" Dio asked his sister.

"I never hear Dad or Mom talking about crazy people here on the *MR*," Jinx answered Dio's question. "You either, now that I think about it."

"You want my opinion?" Guardian Connors, now back in wolf form, asked.

Jinx looked at the Were. "Sure!"

"Ashur is with the Empress. Bellatrix is with Yelena, who dates Bobcat from team BMW, and Dio has Ranger Two as a partner. None of those people spend a lot of time with the ordinary folk here on the *Meredith Reynolds*." Arthur stepped to a container that the ice cream vendor had filled with water and set down for the dogs. After lapping up a few mouthfuls, he turned back to Jinx.

"Your Anne lives an ordinary life. She goes to a regular public school. She doesn't have fame or guards or fear to keep Joe Average away from her," the Were explained.

Jinx snorted. "Anne seems to be earning her own fear factor."

Arthur nodded in understanding. "You might be right, but her combat abilities don't come close to causing the same fear as when the Empress or a Ranger walks into a room.

Jinx thought about it. "That makes sense. You think people are on their best behavior around the others?"

"That," Connors replied, "and the fact that the Empress and the Rangers don't normally deal with the ordinary. They usually deal with people on one end of the spectrum or the other. Either they deal with the elite of society or the dregs."

"Do you think it's worth it?" Jinx asked the Were.

"Being important enough that you don't have to deal with Joe Average?" the Were asked. At Jinx' nod of agreement he continued, "There's not enough money in the universe for me to put up with the crap the Empress has to go through every day."

Dio entered the conversation. "Tabitha has made the same observation."

Jinx chuffed her laughter at the two males. "I guess Anne and I need to quit complaining about the crazies we meet."

CHAPTER FIFTEEN

It was two days before Bethany Anne was able to pull together her fact-finding debrief. Anne, Jinx, and Stevie were shown into a meeting room that had media screens covering two walls.

"Grab a seat." Bethany Anne pointed to some chairs as they entered.

As Anne took one of the indicated seats she waved at Marcus, who had stood when she entered the room. She sat and nodded a greeting to William as Marcus resumed his seat.

Stevie settled into the chair next to Anne's.

"ADAM, would you please run the video footage that you and Seshat have been studying?" Bethany Anne requested.

Everyone was fascinated as the video showed the rubies fly toward each other. There was a flare as the rubies approached each other, and its shape shifted from a disk to a spear as the distance between them diminished. Just before they touched, there was a brighter flash and a sphere of energy shot out. Everyone in the room blinked as the wave front raced toward the camera and the screen went black.

"The energy blast destroyed the camera Seshat was using to record the testing," ADAM announced when the video had ended.

"May we see that again?" Anne requested.

"Sure, ADAM," Bethany Anne prompted.

When the video got to the point where the gems flared Anne called, "Stop, please."

The video froze.

"Would you advance it frame by frame from here?" Anne asked.

"Certainly," ADAM responded, and he displayed the video one frame at a time.

"Stop!" Anne exclaimed as the flare from the rubies morphed from a disk to a spear shape. She got out of her chair and walked to the screen.

"What?" Bethany Anne asked.

"That shape," Anne's finger traced the spear of energy. She looked at Stevie. "It's possible!"

Stevie nodded and Marcus asked, "What's possible?"

"I want to make an energy sword like the ones from the movies. Sort of like Bethany Anne's sword, but one that other people can use," Anne told the scientist. "I wasn't sure before; that's why we were testing. But if we can figure out how to direct the energy to one side of the reaction," Anne's finger traced one side of the energy pattern, "then it could be used without cutting the wielder in two." She ran her finger along the opposite side of the spear. "It just might be possible!"

Bethany Anne stayed quiet until Anne returned to her seat. "That leads us to the next step—finding you research space that won't cause the destruction of the *MR*."

>>Anne, I've been reviewing all the survey data the Yollins did on asteroids in the system, and I think I found the perfect one for our research station.<<

"The Yollins have several mined-out asteroids..." Bethany Anne was explaining.

>>All too large, and without the structural safety we need.<<

"Excuse me?" Anne held up her hand.

"What is it?"

"Those things were strip-mined for their minerals." Anne relayed what she was hearing from Seshat. "They weren't hollowed out with the intention of retaining atmosphere or any concern for whether they'd hold together if there was a large explosion inside them."

"The model I've just run indicates that several of them would come apart if there was a large explosion in their interior space," ADAM told the people in the room.

>>Let them know that there's an asteroid in the survey that is ideal for the situation.<<

"Seshat says that she has come up with an ideal candidate." Anne didn't question Seshat's conclusions, she just reported them to Bethany Anne.

"Oh?" Bethany Anne's right eyebrow rose. "Which one?"

>>Sierra Alpha Four-seven-six-one.<<

"SA Four-seven-six-one," Anne parroted.

"ADAM?" Bethany Anne asked.

"Asteroid Four-seven-six-one was surveyed by the Yollins," ADAM reported to Bethany Anne. "It was shown to have concentrations of valuable metals, but for some reason was never mined."

>>May I speak?<<

"Seshat would like to tap into the room's audio system so she can join the conversation," Anne informed the Empress.

"As long as she doesn't end up in a pissing match with ADAM, fine." Bethany Anne made a "get on with it motion" with her hand.

Seshat said, "Since I didn't have anything better to do, I spent the last two days researching the Yollin asteroid survey reports. The data suggests that the asteroid in question was far enough away that it wouldn't be profitable to ship the mining equipment to it. However, with a few puck engines it should only require five days' travel to place it in a stable orbit behind and outside the *Meredith Reynolds*."

"How do you plan to turn a chunk of solid rock into a research lab?" Bethany Anne was curious to hear Seshat's reply.

"The Empire would advance us the cost of rental for an XR Twenty-one mining machine and a YV Eighteen extruder. I have enough bandwidth to run both machines simultaneously," Seshat claimed. "If the Yollin survey is correct, we can extract enough precious materials to repay the cost of the rentals."

ADAM? Bethany Anne asked.

>>**One second, Bethany Anne.**<< ADAM was silent for two seconds. >>**I haven't searched the data like Seshat apparently has. If the survey figures she just sent me are accurate—and I see no reason the Yollin surveyors would falsify the numbers—at current market prices**

Seshat would break even in thirty-one hours of operation.<<

Nice! Thanks. "I'll get Admiral Thomas to assign someone to move your asteroid, and ADAM will set up a fund Seshat can use to rent the equipment she needs." Bethany Anne smiled as she gave Anne that information, but the smile faded as she continued, "I will require receipts and an expense report, and Seshat will need to check with ADAM if it looks like expenses are going to exceed the funds in the account. Anything else we need to worry about right now?"

Four people shook their heads, so Bethany Anne rose to her feet and clapped her hands once. "Great, let's all head out then."

CHAPTER SIXTEEN

Living in interesting times indeed, Stevie thought as she dodged Jinx' attack. She didn't like to fight, but now she was in a training room with Jinx and Guardian Connors, who were teaching her canine combat techniques.

She'd spent most of her teen years insisting on being called Stevie, yet somehow she hadn't objected when Anne started calling her "Steph."

Stevie yipped as Arthur's claws swiped across her hip, ripping out fur and leaving bloody gashes in their wake.

"Focus!" he growled. "You should never have allowed me to get close enough to do that."

"Sorry," Stevie whined, her ears drooping.

Jinx panted. "If it helps, think that you are trying to protect someone. I pretend I'm protecting Anne, and if I goof up she'll get hurt.

It was thinking about Anne that distracted me in the first place, Stevie thought to herself. She imagined Anne injured, fighting for her life, depending on Stevie to keep enemies off her back.

Jinx and the male Were seemed to shrink and Stevie found herself standing above them. "Huurrttt mmyyyy pacckkk maatttee, willll youuuuu?" the Empire's newest Pricolici howled.

Anne, we need you in Training Room Three like right now! Jinx sent to her person as she dodged the angry monster Stevie had become.

Anne was out with Abby and E, shopping for a little more furniture for her new apartment.

Anne, we need you in Training Room Three like right now! The urgency in Jinx' mind-voice hit her like a slap in the face.

"Hold still!" she ordered her guards, then grabbed them and stepped into the Etheric. She'd been practicing Etheric travel ever since she'd seen what Bethany Anne could do.

Pulling her passengers with her, she shifted her location and peeked out. Crap, this was Room Two. She shifted her location once more and peered out again.

Yep, this was the place. Jinx was dodging a Pricolici. No wonder her call had sounded urgent.

Anne stepped into the training room. She didn't waste time looking at Abby or E, just snapped, "*Stay here!*"

"Hey, Steph, you never told me you could do that." Anne's tone was calm and conversational as she started toward the Pricolici.

Stevie heard the voice of the person she was supposed to be protecting. It sounded normal, not hurt. Stevie stopped swatting at the annoying dog, and when she saw

Anne walking toward her she let go of the wolf she was strangling.

It only took Stevie two bounds to cross to where Anne was. She slid to a stop in front of the girl and sniffed for blood.

What's going on? Anne asked Jinx.

I told her to pretend she was trying to protect someone, and she shifted into that and mentioned us hurting a packmate. I think she imagined you *getting hurt, and somehow this form doesn't let her separate imagination from reality.*

"Look, I'm all right," Stevie's pack leader said as she held out her arms and turned in a circle. "But I'm not hugging you while you're seven feet tall and have daggers for fingernails."

Stevie looked at her hands, *Oh, no shit,* she thought when she saw the four-inch-long claws. Suddenly Stevie felt the cool air of the training room on her skin, and she looked down at herself in shock. She was standing in front of Anne naked, as in having no clothes on.

Anne was a little surprised to find Stevie in front of her in her birthday suit, but she tried her best to act as if it were completely natural. Steph had obviously stressed out over something, and she didn't need more dumped on her right now. "That's better," Anne remarked, and opened her arms. She had to kneel, because with a muttered "Crap" Stevie shifted into wolf form.

She wrapped her arms around Stevie's furry neck. "Are you okay?" Anne felt the nod on her shoulder.

"Can we talk about this somewhere other than here?" Stevie's wolf whined at her.

Anne was pleased to discover that whatever it was about her that had allowed her to understand Ashur, back when they first met, seemed to work for Weres in wolf form. "No problem," Anne confirmed. "Let's all head back to my place, and I'll ask Sergeant Wendville to send over some food.

Abby had taken the guard position briefly so her cousin E could grab a quick bite, then Abby and Arthur had headed to the mess, leaving E on duty at Anne's new apartment.

Anne licked the grease and salt from her fingers. She didn't do it often, but today she had just felt like some fish and chips. She didn't think the Yollin fish and potato equivalents were as good as they were on Earth, but she was willing to admit her memory of the fish and chip cart in the casino might have been faulty.

Jinx had already finished her steak, so Anne waited as Stevie mopped up the last of the sauce from her double order of spaghetti and meatballs with her garlic toast.

"You feel up to talking about what happened?" Anne asked as Stevie pushed her empty container away and sat back with a contented sigh.

"It's a little embarrassing." Stevie blushed, looking anywhere but at Anne.

"She kept losing focus during training," Jinx related. "I told her I pretended I had to protect you to motivate myself, and suggested she imagine needing to protect someone to see if the same thing could help her. Next thing we knew, she'd shifted to that big form and had poor Arthur by the throat. As long as I ran around her and barked, it distracted her enough that she didn't try to do any further damage to him. I kept running so she couldn't turn me into the doggy version of hamburger and called you for help."

Stevie sighed, and finally managed to look Anne in the face. "I used Jinx' suggestion and thought of you," she confessed. "In my mind, you had been injured because I hadn't been able to protect you. Next thing I knew I was a monster, and screaming at Jinx and Guardian Connors."

Anne leaned close enough to pat Stevie on the knee. "First, you weren't a monster!" she said emphatically. "From everything I've heard while training with Peter, it's a rare and special ability. You will just need to practice so you can control your emotions in that form. Apparently it's easy to go berserk, and then we'd have problems."

"I'm not sure I want to do that again," Stevie proclaimed.

Anne sighed and looked at the Were sympathetically. "That's not surprising," she told her friend, "but you need to learn to control it, so it doesn't control you."

"You could practice here," Jinx suggested. "That way no one else would see you shift."

Stevie was quiet for a moment while she thought about

Jinx' suggestion, then she nodded. "That would be workable."

"Great, we have a plan of action!" Anne smiled at Jinx, then Stevie.

"I hate to interrupt," Seshat's avatar said from the previously blank monitor, "but ADAM has just informed me our asteroid has arrived."

FINIS

AUTHOR NOTES - STEPHEN RUSSELL

AUGUST 7, 2017

Again, huge heartfelt thanks to all of you who have made it this far!

I was completely blown away by the success of *Etheric Recruit*. I hope you have enjoyed *Etheric Researcher* as much.

Writing about Jinx and writing scenes from her perspective is both challenging and fun. I've been blessed with the company of several amazingly smart dogs over my lifetime. It's taken a lot of years, but I finally learned that I was allowing my limited expectations to control what I tried to teach my dogs. I've found it to be absolutely amazing what a dog is capable of learning as long as their human is capable of teaching them. Luckily for me Jinx is well mannered. So, I won't have to write scenes where she's gotten hold of a role of paper towel and shredded it into quarter sized pieces scattered all over the living room floor. (True story, it looked like it had snowed in the house!)

I have a confession, after several hours immersed in

writing or editing scenes with *Seshat*, there were two occasions I called my Amazon device, *Seshat*. It doesn't answer to that, go figure.

AUTHOR NOTES - MICHAEL ANDERLE

WRITTEN NOVEMBER 30, 2017

WOW!

First, THANK YOU for reading these author notes where we get a chance to wax philosophically, or just say random stuff.

Either is good sometimes.

I remember when Stephen called me up ready to talk beats for this book. I was in Las Vegas, walking down a sidewalk towards Las Vegas Blvd (the strip) from the Aria hotel. I ended up talking to him on my phone walking up and down the sidewalk in front of the VEER towers for like thirty-five minutes.

I'm happy the weather was pleasant that day.

This is Stephen's second book, and typically, an indie author doesn't need to stress too much about their sopho-more effort. While I'm fairly successful now, my first book was *NOT* successful like Stephen's.

Since he won't speak too much about himself (and I will, since he won't see these notes until after they are placed online for everyone to read) I want to admit that his success with Anne and Jinx is CRAZY!

He rose to first place in a YA genre category and he didn't come down for WEEKS. It just kept selling and selling and selling and making fans happy.

I told him I should have written a book with a dog in it.

Then we both realized I had (Ashur) but he doesn't show up for a few books and I didn't put him front and center on the cover until Never Forsaken (Book 05).

Now, Stephen's life has come full circle as the production editor is now the successful author.

I'm happy you like these characters and Stephen's stories.

I would like to personally thank *you* for supporting a man who gave of his time and talents to willingly help me a year and a half ago. Your support has brought to reality what was just a dream for Stephen before.

Now he not only has one book out, he has two. In the reviews for this book, why don't you ask him when book 03 is coming out?

It would serve him right for all of those times he gave me sh#t when you fans gave me a hard time.

May he write many more stories that entertain us all far into the future.

Ad Aeternitatem,

Michael Anderle

p.s. Stephen – Now YOU get to know what it feels like to have a character (a dog) that can't die. Because if he dies, you will have a TON of very unhappy dog-loving readers.

OTHER BOOKS BY SR RUSSELL

WANT MORE KURTHERIAN GAMBIT?

Website:
http://www.lmbpn.com

Email List:
http://lmbpn.com/email/

Facebook Here:
www.facebook.com/TheKurtherianGambitBooks/